Further Studies In Statecraft

The Political Memoirs Of Mycroft Holmes

The Redacted Novels III

Orlando Pearson

Hardcover ISBN 978-1-80424-727-3
Paperback ISBN 978-1-80424-728-0
ePub ISBN 978-1-80424-729-7
PDF ISBN 978-1-80424-730-3

Published by MX Publishing
335 Princess Park Manor, Royal Drive,
London, N11 3GX
www.mxpublishing.co.uk

Cover design Awan

Contents

Introduction by Henry Durham, historical advisor to *The Redacted Sherlock Holmes* series

The first collection of Mycroft's Holmes's edited papers was published as *A Study in Statecraft* in 2023.

I had discovered the papers by complete chance when I was researching the cricketing exploits of the 19th century Mycroft brothers at the Public Record Office at Kew. I had previously discovered Dr Watson's private papers in the same archives, and they have formed the basis of *The Redacted Sherlock Holmes* series, so called as they included works so sensitive in nature that they could not be published at the same time as the canonical works.

Further Studies in Statecraft contains another selection of the Mycroft Holmes papers and could similarly never have been published until the events that they refer to had become the stuff of history books. It is not too much to say that some of the revelations contained in this collection of Mycroft Holmes's writing and in the previous one will cause those same history books to be rewritten.

It is important for readers to bear in mind when reading these works, that while Mycroft Holmes never excluded the possibility of his papers being published, he regarded his writings as a series of case studies in statecraft and not as works designed to entertain the public. This explains the dry style of his own narration. This style is leavened by the crowd-pleasing prose of Dr Watson in several of the works both in this collection and in the previous volume of Mycroft's memoirs. Mycroft makes it clear in frequent observations that, like his brother, he disapproves of what he sees as Watson's romanticising of events.

My main role as editor of these papers has been to:

☐ Provide an afterword to five of the six episodes contained here, although not to *A Question of Paternity* where Dr Watson's closing comments seemed definitive enough without any further elucidation;

☐ Add notes on what sums of money at the times of these works are worth in the money of 2025; and

☐ Create the cover and add portraits to the text – thus, the small pictures of people on the cover and in places within the body of the text are, unless otherwise stated, my own additions to what Mycroft left. The few exceptions to this are instances where Mycroft Holmes himself included pictures appended to his text.

The pictures within the text are identified there and the pictures on the cover, apart from Mycroft Holmes on the right, are (from top left) Captain Alfred Dreyfus, German Field-Marshal Erhard Milch, Unity Mitford, a contemporary cartoon portrayal of the Ripper killer, Winston Churchill, Hermann Göring, and the White House.

What of the statecraft on display here?

One of the reviewers of these works has said that the Mycroft who emerges from his papers is utterly unscrupulous.

Mycroft contrasts himself with his brother in *L'Affaire Dreyfus* in which, unusually for this collection, both brothers appear, and Mycroft writes as follows:

> My brother remains motivated by a love of truth and justice.
>
> For my part I see it as my responsibility to seek political advantage for this country.
>
> Truth and justice, while doubtless very worthy things, must sometimes take second place to the pursuit of national advantage, and, while the objectives might coincide, it is perfectly possible for them to clash as they do here.

As the reader will discover, when there is a clash, Mycroft is on the side of Realpolitik. This causes him to make decisions not everyone will approve of and which some will profoundly disagree with.

Mycroft cites as his main influence the Florentine political writer, Niccolò Machiavelli, whose masterpieces, *The Prince* and *The Art of War*, inform much of the statecraft on display here.

There is no political colour in Mycroft's scheming which may explain why he was Chief Permanent Advisor to Prime Ministers of all political persuasions. In this volume he is consulted by a future Conservative Prime Minister, Winston Churchill, and he was consulted by two serving Liberal Prime Ministers, Herbert Asquith and David Lloyd George, in the previous volume.

Mycroft's own political strategy is quite simple.

☐ He wishes above all else that Great Britain enjoys political stability in the account of *The Ripper and his Master.*

☐ He is of the view that this country's interests are best served by having France and Germany locked in a cycle of mutual suspicion as this lessens the chances of Britain's continental rivals uniting against this country.

This belief informs his conduct of *L'Affaire Dreyfus* of 1894/5 and *A Case of Paternity* of 1935, indeed in the latter work he regards Hermann Göring's decision to put pragmatism over racial dogma with grave foreboding.

☐ He is a free-trader and negotiates a favourable trading treaty with the Americans in *Liberation Day* in a work which describes events which are of great historical interest, but which could not conceivably recur in modern times.

☐ In *Some Taxing Matters* he smooths the path for Winston Churchill's continued political career and in *Eva and the Woman from Swastika* he averts an acute political embarrassment, another example of his desire to keep the ship of state moving forward smoothly.

In the fifty or so years running up to the latest work in this collection in which the events took place at the end of 1939, Mycroft receives some extraordinary visitors either to his quarters in Pall Mall or at the Diogenes Club conveniently located just opposite.

He grants audiences to the future King Edward VII in the 1880s and to French President Jean Casimir-Perier in the 1890s. As well as Winston Churchill, humourist PG Wodehouse calls on him in *Some Taxing Matters*, while Hitler's companion, Eva Braun, consults in the penultimate work in this collection, *Eva and the Woman from Swastika*, from the second half of 1939.

The work of sorting through the copious writings of Mycroft Holmes is as yet incomplete and this will not be the last set of works under the *Study in Statecraft* imprint.

Henry Durham

London 2025

The Ripper and his Master

Introduction by Mycroft Holmes

I impounded the text below by Dr Watson.

If any future readers should have the opportunity to read it, they will discover that my brother plays only the most minor role in the matter it relates.

Dr Watson made no protests about this work's confiscation, perhaps realising that a work such as this which presents an unresolved case and which did not showcase the somewhat meretricious skills of young Sherlock, was of little commercial value.

The events described underline the supremacy of *raison d'état*.

If the reader sees some of the *Realpolitik* of Niccolò Machiavelli behind the statecraft described, then that is not something I am ashamed of.

Part One

The Ripper

Being a recollection by Dr John Watson

It seems extraordinary.

The best-known crime in the world took place at a time and in a city where the greatest detective of all time was at work. And yet the records that have come down to us do not even mention my friend in relation to it. As my readers will discover as they read my account of events, there is a very good and simple reason for this, but it seems only right to start at the beginning.

It was just as I was about to get up for breakfast on the morning of the 8th of September 1888 that Holmes tapped on my door.

"Truly," I heard him say from the corridor outside my room, "the world is a changing place. Brother Mycroft is here, and he says he wants to see me urgently. It must be a matter of the utmost seriousness for him to disrupt his routine. And for a matter important enough to bring my brother here, I would not wish to be without my Boswell. He is waiting for us down in the sitting room. There is no need to shave before you see him."

I quickly dressed and was downstairs in a few minutes.

"As I was saying before you bolted through the door to fetch Dr Watson from upstairs, dear Sherlock, I would prefer it, if we could consult in private. This is a matter of the utmost secrecy," I heard Mycroft say as I sat down in the little sitting-room.

I rose at once to leave, but Holmes also rose, and he pushed me back down into my seat. "Both or none," said he, turning to his brother.

"Oh, very well, dear Sherlock, if you insist," came Mycroft's grudging reply, "we will discuss the matter I would wish to raise with both of you present."

"So, what is it?" asked Holmes, and I too was agog as to what Mycroft was going to say.

"Photography," said Mycroft simply.

"Photography?" asked Holmes, looking baffled in a way I was not used to seeing.

"Indeed, good Sherlock. A Mr Eastman of Rochester near New York has registered a patent for a camera which carries a roll of film and so can take multiple pictures before they need to be developed."

Mycroft stopped as though he expected some sort of reaction, but nothing seemed to occur to his brother, and I too was at a loss as to where this was leading.

"Well," said Mycroft, looking puzzled that neither of us was more engaged, "do you not see the potential for this in espionage? At present a spy can only take one picture at a time and then it must be developed. Or he must carry multiple cameras around with him. Now one camera can take multiple images meaning more images can be taken and the photography is much more portable. I want you to go to Rochester, Sherlock, and explore the potential of this invention. This country has a first-rate espionage service, but we are not the only country with a secret service, and I want to make sure our spies have the best equipment at their disposal as soon as possible. No less than the defence of our realm depends on it. Now is the time to go as the patent has only just been filed."

I think my friend was only mildly impressed by this proposition, but he asked, "What limits are there on my actions once I am there?"

"To enable this country to make the most of this technical advance, dear brother, your scope is unlimited. If you can stay on the side of the law, then pray do so. If you need to break into Mr Eastman's factory, purloin his intellectual property, and see what other powers are aware of this development – I am sure your exposure to criminal work will have made you an accomplished burglar, not to mention impersonator and pugilist – then you will be covered by diplomatic privilege and we will make sure that any local interest in bringing charges against you is thwarted."

"And when do you want us to go?"

"I fear this commission is only for you, dear Sherlock and so there is no 'us'. The Prime Minister sees this as highly speculative, and was reluctant to pay for anyone else to go. And you are likely to be in the United States for a considerable amount of time. I cannot see the need or the desirability for a chronicler in what is a mission of espionage against a friendly state. And as for the timing, I would like you to be on your way as soon as possible before others become aware of this invention and realise its potential."

I think my friend was slightly sceptical about what he was being asked to do but he had no other case on and in the end he went to pack a bag. When he returned Mycroft said, "I will accompany you to Paddington for the train to Bristol where a ship sails at three o'clock this afternoon so that I can brief you further. You will be in Rochester within a week. There is no need to keep me informed while you are there for I fear that any communications from you may be intercepted by rival states anxious to get hold of this extraordinary technological advance."

Holmes and Mycroft were soon gone.

I went back upstairs and shaved before I sat down to breakfast alone. I then turned my attention to the newspapers in which there was nothing of any great interest. I was wondering what to do until lunchtime when Inspector Lestrade arrived.

"I was hoping to find Mr Holmes here," he said.

It struck me that Lestrade was not sounding himself and when I looked at him more closely I noted that he looked far from well. It was not my habit to ask after Lestrade's health, but I did so now.

He wiped his brow and said, "Well, Dr Watson, I have seen a body mutilated in a way I have never seen before and hope never to see again. I've just come from there. It's why I want to see Mr Holmes."

Once again I now did something I never did at any other time and brought Lestrade some brandy which he swallowed in one gulp.

"Trust a doctor to know the right treatment," said he, some colour returning to his cheeks.

His downcast look re-appeared when I said, "I fear Mr Holmes is away. He is bound for the United States, and I have no idea when he will be back."

"Well, there's a blow and no mistake," said Lestrade, his voice filled with gloom. "It's like this," he went on. "I have just come from Whitechapel. A woman there…"

"What sort of woman?" I asked.

"…well, the sort of woman we would normally refer to as 'an unfortunate', has been disembowelled and her innards pulled right out over her shoulder. Her throat had been cut right across. It may be, and it would be a mercy if it were so – yes, Dr Watson, another shot of brandy would be just what I need – that she was dead from having her throat cut before the rest happened."

"Where was this?"

"In Hanbury Street. The worst part of London. The whole area is a den of gin, opium, and poor women making a living by selling themselves just to be able to afford the fourpence (*Note by Henry Durham*: about £2 or USD 2.50 in 2025 money) for a bed for the night in one of the common lodging houses."

"Are murders in that part of London and in that class of people not quite common?"

"What you say, Dr Watson, is of course true", said Lestrade thoughtfully. "Before this case we had had had three murders of unfortunates in Whitechapel since April. One was a killing by a gang. We can't prove anything, but she was probably killed on the instructions of the man she worked for. The other two were killed and mutilated. One of the ones whose body had been mutilated had had her throat cut as well. It's early days yet but it is a reasonable suspicion that the one whose throat was cut and body ripped was killed by the same person as did the killing I have just come from."

"So, I take it you have not apprehended the killers in any of these cases?"

"We have not. Conducting any sort of investigation and getting reliable witnesses are both real difficulties in that part of the world."

"So why has this murder so disturbed you? Surely in your line of work you have seen much similar."

"I have not, Dr Watson. I have seen many, many corpses, God knows, but this is much the worst mutilation of a body I have ever seen and the woman whose throat was cut a few weeks ago was also badly slashed all over."

"And do you have nothing to go on?"

"When I left the crime scene we had been able to identify no one at all who had seen or heard anything at all."

"Could the fact that the woman's throat had been cut have prevented her screaming?"

"That is very likely so Dr Watson. The knife was plunged so deep into her throat that the vertebrae of her backbone were scored by the tip of the blade."

"And has no one reported hearing a struggle?"

"You would have thought that people – it's a very densely populated neighbourhood – would have heard that but no one yet come forward."

"Have the doctors come up with anything? If a throat is cut, you should at least be able to tell whether the person who struck the blow is lefthanded or righthanded."

Lestrade looked rather struck by this thought.

"The throat was slit was from the victim's left to right. And for what the two of them were likely to have been up to, it is probable that the killer struck from behind – that's the way it works on the street. That means the killer was righthanded – which, unfortunately does not much narrow our search – but the question you have posed is a good one, Dr Watson."

He again looked rather thoughtful and lit a cigar which he sat smoking for several minutes without saying a word.

"Are you busy at the moment, Dr Watson?"

In those early days I had no occupation at all other than to assist my friend on his cases. My only income came from my army pension and Holmes had to pay for any major expenditure. This was why I had not been able to join Holmes in America in a private capacity as an Atlantic crossing would have been beyond my pocket as well as that of Holmes. And Holmes was now away *sine die* so the days ahead stretched before me with nothing to capture my interest. I said as much to Lestrade.

"I wonder, Doctor, if you would care to provide your medical insight on this matter. Our police doctors take a dismissive view of cases that involve these so-called unfortunates. And our mortuary staff have the habit of stealing sellable organs from the deceased for medical research."

"They do what?" asked I, scarce able to believe what I had heard.

"It's poorly paid work that they do and it's how they make a turn. That's why it would be good to have a medical man take a fresh pair of eyes to this. And you can charge Scotland Yard what you see fit for your experience as a doctor. It is much easier to justify paying a doctor than paying a consultant with no direct qualifications like Mr Holmes."

I considered the Inspector's proposition and saw no reason to turn it down. I postponed my lunch and set off with Lestrade.

"It's a grim place where it happened. Mostly people live in boarding houses. The men pay for it by doing casual work at the docks, the women by selling their favours."

At this point we were going down Gower Street with the white Portland stone of University College on the left and fine townhouses on the right. "You know, Dr Watson," said Lestrade, "in London a third of women are respectably married, a third are in service, and a third routinely sell themselves to make ends meet. That is the choice, if you can call it that, that they have, though of course, some do two or even three of those things at various times or sometimes even at the same time. Another ten minutes and we'll be in East London."

"I have not been there for a long time."

"It's full of the poorest people from all over the world. Lots of people who can't make a living in Ireland. And lots of Jews who've been driven from Russia by... what are they called?" Lestrade came to a halt as he thought about the word he was looking for.

"Pogroms?" I suggested – I only know the word from the reports I has read about in that morning's newspapers of another of these waves of expulsion and expropriation which seemed to afflict Eastern Europe with such frequency and such brutish consequences.

"That's the word, Doctor," confirmed Lestrade. "And there are more Laskars – sailors of Indian origin – than you can imagine."

The streets got narrower and dirtier as we got beyond St Paul's. We rattled past a brick- built church.

"That's St Botolph's," said Lestrade. "That's where the women parade around to get business."

I looked out and was surprised to see a column of women whose occupation was clear walking round the church as if to confirm Lestrade's words.

"Is this business still going on in spite of the killings?" I asked in some surprise.

"Well, it's daylight now," said Lestrade, "so they probably feel safer but actually there are more of them out now than there were because there are fewer punters. The news of the murder will have got around and that will scare people off, so the women have to be out more often and for longer. They probably charge less as well. It will be much busier here at night even though that is when the killer strikes."

"And there are lots of coaches," I observed. "I am surprised to see that in so poor an area."

Lestrade gave a rueful chuckle.

"You are much likelier to see a coach than a bicycle round here. Most of the women live in work-houses or boarding houses where they cannot go to with clients. It is only few who have permanent accommodation. So, most of the trade takes place outside down some God-forsaken alley. The better class of client comes by coach and takes the woman on board. You'll note none of the coaches have any identifying mark to tell you who is inside them."

Even as we watched, the coach in front of us stopped and one of the women standing on the pavement sprang in. A little further down the road on the other side, another coach come to a halt and a ragged lad of about fifteen got out. He stood at the window of the carriage, gave the occupant inside a cheery wave, and then did a cartwheel on the street before standing upright once more. As we rumbled past him, I could see him stood at the kerb with his arm raised in a florid salute as the carriage drove off.

"You get all sorts here," grunted Lestrade. "I should really arrest him, but I don't see the point." He looked around, "It's actually quite quiet. It gets much busier at night."

We were soon at the police morgue and Lestrade pulled on the handle of a drawer which opened to reveal a body on a slab.

"She was called Annie Chapman," said he.

I have taken the decision in writing this account not to dwell on the condition of any of the cadavers that I saw and will say no more here other than that I could understand Inspector Lestrade's reaction at what he had seen earlier that day.

I performed an analysis of the wounds and was able to establish that they had been inflicted by a very sharp knife – as opposed to a cut-throat razor which would have been sharp enough but which would not have inflected a wound of the depth I saw or a bayonet which would have got the depth but which would not have been sharp enough to rip out the throat or carry out the rest of the mutilations. The knife's thin blade must have been six to eight inches long. Where, I mused, could the murderer have got hold of such a knife. A surgeon, I speculated, could get hold of any sort of blade and handle he wanted though what would a surgeon be doing among drink-sozzled unfortunates? A leather-worker might have a knife of the requisite sharpness but not, I fancied, the length of blade. A slaughter-house worker or butcher might be a better candidate. When I examined the lungs of the victim, alas all too easy given the state of the body, I could see that they were degraded to an extent that would have caused her death in the next few months.

After I had completed my examination and given my thoughts to Lestrade, there was nothing left to do so I returned to Baker Street. Accounts started appearing on the newspapers of the spate of killings and of the reaction of people living in the

East End who turned first on Irish and then on Jewish migrants as the newspapers started speculating that the gruesome killings were part of a Jewish ritual. There was one report of an anti-Jewish riot which was something I had only previously read about in reports about foreign countries.

It was in the small hours of the 30th of September that the next development came. I was woken at half-past-three in the morning by a frantic-looking Lestrade.

"There's been another one," he said. By the light of his lantern, I could see he was wild-eyed with horror. I dressed as fast as I could and then we rattled through the black streets of London – by the time this is read, if it ever is, my readers may have forgotten that in 1888 London was almost completely unlit – and by a quarter past four we were at what I was told was Berner Street. "There's a yard off the street at number forty. It's the sort of place where a woman takes her client."

Lestrade held up his lantern and in the pool of light it cast I could see that the latest victim had had her throat cut from left to right just like Annie Chapman.

"But she has not been mutilated," I said, looking at the body.

"We think the killer was disturbed, This is the home of one Louis Diemschutz, and he discovered the body when he drove into this yard to park up his horse and cart."

"Does that mean the killer was in this yard when the body was discovered?"

"It is hard to say. A horse and cart ratting down the street is a common enough sound around here so the killer probably would not have known it would turn in here but maybe he sensed it and bolted just before the cart arrived. And of-course Diemschutz will have had no more light than we have so hiding in the shadows would have been easy."

"Do we know who she…"

But before I could get the question out, a panic-filled voice rang out of the blackness beyond Lestrade's lantern, "There's another woman been killed, Inspector."

We followed what proved to be a young constable. At moments like these it is hard to track the time, but I would say it was no more than twenty minutes before we were at what I was told was called Mitre Square.

Again by Lestrade's lantern, for there was no other source of light, I could see the victim's throat had been cut from left to right and this time there had been no disturbance to the killer at his work for here the body had been ripped asunder – I know no other phrase that will do and I will provide no more details of what I saw as this is a work of record rather than a romance to titillate the depraved.

"What is this?" gasped Lestrade, who had been confronted with the work of this killer even more than I. "This is as bad as the first two cases."

"I'm the beat policeman for around here and I came through the square but a quarter of an hour before the body was found. I saw nothing untoward then," came the voice which by the light of another lantern I could see came from another young constable. "This must have happened in the twinkling of eye, and yet no one has heard anything."

"Our killer has powers that are barely human," came Lestrade's voice. "He can strike in seconds and no one – in any of the cases we are looking at and in this, the most overcrowded part of London – no one hears a thing."

"Sir! Sir!" an insistent voice from the darkness, "we've found something."

"Not a third body?" asked Lestrade, sounding beaten.

"No sir, we have found a piece of the other woman's clothing in a doorway and there is some writing chalked on the wall above it. I will take you there."

I think there was a feeling of relief that we would not be looking at another murder victim and Lestrade and I ran after the young officer who was carrying a lantern.

I mentioned in *The Hound of the Baskerville*, the events of which occurred in the autumn of the year following the events I now describe, that I am regarded as fleet of foot. As I was to do on Dartmoor a year later, I soon outpaced Lestrade, and arrived panting at Goulston Street. At a tenement there was a group of four policeman led by what I can only describe as a particularly burly and bearded member of the constabulary in a senior officer's uniform with a peaked cap over his eyes. With his girth and beard, he bore a passing resemblance to the Prince of Wales, Albert Edward, I thought. He was standing in the light of a single lantern held high by a tall constable. I saw a piece of scrawly writing on the wall.

What I write below is what a constable subsequently gave to Lestrade.

> "The Juwes are the men that Will not be Blamed for nothing".

As my reader will note that if the second word refers to Jews, the spelling is one that is not generally used. My own reading of the text had Juives rather than Juwes. Juives is the French plural of Jewesses, but this makes no sense in a sentence in English making a specific reference to men. The scrawl admitted to either version.

Even as I watched, the leading officer said to his junior colleagues in a rather curious high-pitched voice and with an accent I could not place, "As the most senior man here, I have taken the decision that this message must be washed off. I have made sure its content is noted down, and I am of the view that it is liable to create a disturbance if it is more widely seen. One anti-Jewish riot is enough."

A bucket of water was fetched from inside the house and the writing was obliterated just as Lestrade came panting up behind me. As he did so the burly officer at the top of the tenement entry steps suddenly seemed to collapse before our eyes, falling forward and down the stairs, toppling into his lantern-bearing colleague who in turn fell into another colleague so that they all fell over like nine-pins. I heard the lantern smash on the ground with a crash of metal and the tinkling of glass. We were plunged into the blackest darkness. It took several minutes of fumbling around before another lantern could be lit. When we once again had some light, it was to my astonishment that I found that the burly senior officer – he had been a superintendent I was told – had vanished into thin air.

"Well, who was he?" I heard Lestrade ask his brother officers.

"We don't know everyone in the police force. And officers come and go," came the slightly sulky sounding voice of one of the constables. "He walked the walk of a superintendent, and he talked the talk. And it's dark."

"So you had not taken the precaution of checking his identity and establishing that he was who he said he was?"

Silence.

"So he may have been the killer or an associate of the killer? And he has obliterated our best piece of evidence," persisted Lestrade.

"He's too big and too clumsy to be a killer who tours the streets killing in silence and disappearing into thin air. And we don't know that the writing had anything to do with the killing."

Silence.

There seemed nothing more to say and Lestrade and I walked back to Mitre Square with Lestrade chuntering, "A tall fat man in a superintendent's uniform. It doesn't make any sense. And invisible. Yet, we have nothing else to go on!"

Formalities complete at Mitre Square, I was back at Baker Street soon after daybreak, and wondered how many more cases there might be. If we assumed that of the killings before Annie Chapman, only the woman who had had her throat cut was killed by the same person as had killed the other three, that still meant that there were four women who had been killed and mutilated in the most horrific way imaginable. Yet no one had heard them or seen anything. Our only suspect was a superintendent who had none of the characteristics of a silent killer and even he, in spite of his girth, seemed to have disappeared without trace.

My readers may suspect, as I did, that Sherlock Holmes would not have been so in the dark as Lestrade appeared to be. The ferrety-face inspector came round regularly – I think in the hope that I may have some news of when my friend might return, not that Holmes would have troubled to tell me that he was on his way. Finally, he said, "Mr Holmes always said I should lock myself up in a library and look at past criminal cases for ideas. Could I, Dr Watson, look at your notes of the cases you have conducted with Mr Holmes? In the absence of the man himself, his cases might give me some ideas."

I somewhat reluctantly got my casebook out and the inspector pored over it.

"I have it!" he exclaimed. "Toby!"

Toby was the name of the dog we had used as a tracker in *The Sign of Four* which, in the version I published, took place at precisely this time, autumn 1888, but in fact occurred a little earlier. The change to its dating was made at the specific request of Mycroft who did not want Holmes's absence from what became known as the Ripper case left unexplained. "Far better," Mycroft had said, "that people think my brother was doing something else than that he was beaten by this or that they might explain his absence by speculating he might have been on an espionage mission which is precisely what he is doing at present."

"A killer cannot fail to leave behind a trail of his scent," said Lestrade, warming to his idea, "even if he cannot be seen or heard. If there is another killing, I will use dogs to lead me to the killer."

The next time Lestrade came round, he was, to the visible displeasure of Mrs Hudson, in the company of two bloodhounds – Burgho and Barnaby.

"We have policemen everywhere in Whitechapel," he said, rubbing his hands together, "and if my men can't catch the killer, these two will sniff him out. He'll not escape me."

And yet we had a while to wait.

October passed, mercifully without any outrages, and I had started to wonder whether the killer had been apprehended on another offence or been confined to an asylum or come to grief in some other unconnected matter.

Then in the early afternoon of Friday the 9th of November I got a message from Lestrade. "Come to 13 Miller's Court, behind 26 Dorset Street, Spitalfields at once."

I got there to find Lestrade waiting for me.

"I have the dogs arriving shortly but it's another one."

We went inside.

I hope I have given the reader an insight into what this killer did with the bodies without being ghoulish, but this was many times worse than anything we had seen before.

"We think the killer had more time," speculated Lestrade. "The woman was called Mary Kelly, and she operated from this room. Our theory is she admitted someone who she thought was a client and was attacked."

"I have never seen a body look worse than this even after the most grievous wounds on the battlefield," I commented. "And I see the killer has set fire to her clothing."

"That may have been to provide light to do what he did."

"And no one saw or heard anything?"

"No."

There was a tap on the door.

"The dogs are here, sir," said a sergeant.

"At least after something like this, there must be a trail," said Lestrade and we went out into the grey autumn early afternoon.

The dogs looked as frisky as I could imagine, and we were off. They strained at their leashes as we entered Dorset Street, and I felt a surge of hope that we might be onto something. They turned confidently into Crispin Street and then one wanted to stay on the same side of the road while the other ardently wished to cross it.

"We'll follow each scent and see where they take us," said Lestrade.

We had gone no further than another hundred yards up Crispin Street when the dogs turned back on themselves, and we retraced our steps.

"We should have taken the other trail," said Lestrade but instead the dogs continued determinedly past where the other trail was and turned into Brushfield Street. A few minutes more and we turned back into Dorset Street to end up back at the point where we had started.

By four it was getting dark, and we had made no further progress.

"We'll get him yet," said Lestrade, his determination apparently unabated, though I saw no means how, and I made my way back to Baker Street.

A week later Holmes came through the door.

He was weighed down with luggage but looked downcast.

"It was only on the ship back that I was able to read British newspapers and find out what had happened here in my absence. A killer strikes at will and I am detained out of the country."

I gave my friend a questioning look.

"I got to Rochester in five days," he said. "I confess I had been slightly sceptical of my brother's commission from the first, but I was able to buy cameras at the factory shop which, I was able to establish, could take multiple pictures through a new kind of film which replaced the plate that normal cameras have."

He paused and lit a cigarette.

"I took these cameras to my hotel and did my best to examine the mechanical means whereby the film moved and then to look at the chemistry of the materials used."

"And what did you find?"

"My activities were severely circumscribed by the lack of laboratory facilities."

"Could you not have applied at Rochester's university?"

"I looked into it but the only laboratory that they had is named after Mr Eastman, the inventor of this new type of camera, so I felt that if I hired space to examine cameras, it would excite comment."

"So what did you do?"

"I decided in the end, good Watson, that the easiest solution was to break into the Eastman factory and so elucidate the techniques and technology that was being used."

"And?"

"I broke in on a Friday evening so that I would have the full weekend to work. I found my way to Mr Eastman's private office. I noted a burn hole on the carpet in front of a picture and realised that it had been caused by ash that had fallen from a cigar as someone stood for an extended period in front of it. I deduced that this was where Mr Eastman stood to open the safe and removal of the picture confirmed my inference. I had surmised that this was what would hold the details of the company's processes, and I had brought my safe-cracking equipment with me. I was working on it when the office-door opened, and an armed guard came in followed by another. My focus had been on the safe and against such odds resistance was pointless. An hour later and I found myself in Rochester's gaol."

My friend paused and I waited for a story of a dramatic gaol break or an unexpected means of getting what he wanted from within the gaol. Instead, Holmes continued, "I have been detained there ever since, and it was only due to the kind but not over-swift engagement of the British ambassador that I am free now. I was able to bring my cameras back, but I am returned with only what was publicly available, although I would be happy to give my brother the benefit of my research into these devices."

At this moment there was the sound of a tread – no, two treads – on the stairs.

"I had a man watch this house so I could come here as soon as you were back, Mr Holmes," said Lestrade as he came through the door. "We need your help for a series of murders."

Almost at the same time Mycroft said, "I heard from the British ambassador that you were on your way, Sherlock. Inspection of the times of liners to Bristol and trains from there, enabled me to infer when you would arrive here."

Lestrade briefed my friend on the series of horrific murders in Whitechapel, but he had barely got to the end when Mycroft broke in insistently to ask about the cameras. My friend was forced to postpone any questions he might have had for Lestrade to explain the workings and possible uses of the new sorts of camera.

Rather to my surprise for a man who was supposed to be investigating crimes that had taken place in the blackness of an unlit East End, it was Lestrade who looked most interested, "I wonder," interjected he, "whether we could use these new types of cameras to photograph the eyes of the victims to see whether they recorded what their attacker looked like."

"That sounds an excellent idea," said Mycroft.

Almost at the same time his brother said, "But that is like photographing a mirror after the object you want to photograph has stopped being reflected by it."

"And all the killings occurred in the dark," I added.

"Not Mary Kelly," came back the answer from Lestrade. "The killer burnt her clothes to dismember her. Well, she's the latest victim so her body is the freshest. And, in any case, I have no other idea at present of how to investigate this matter," he added a little sulkily.

"I think, good brother," said Mycroft, "it would be useful if Inspector Lestrade took these cameras to see what use he can make of them in his investigation."

"I will go to the morgue now. No time to waste," said Lestrade and made for the door.

"Perhaps, Inspector, you might brief my brother on your results when the exercise is complete."

In not many minutes more, the flat was empty of visitors leaving Sherlock Holmes and me sat at our usual station on either side of the hearth.

Readers who are acquainted with the minutiae of the events I have described will know that while other murders of unfortunates took place in Whitechapel after this grim day in November 1888, none bore the horrific characteristics of the four I have described in some detail and the first one which I have referred to as having the same characteristics.

The trail had gone too cold even for my friend who lamented his absence from London while such outré events were afoot.

For my part I spent my time redating the events described in what became *The Sign of Four* as I prepared my manuscript for publication.

The Ripper And his Master

Being a recollection by Mycroft Holmes

I pen these words which set out for the first time in writing what I know about the Whitechapel Killings which are also known as the Ripper killings. I do so in a state of some doubt about my moral compass even though these words are being put to paper decades after the event. As I write as the man who *is* the British Government, any future reader will be unsurprised to learn that I know more than anyone else about it.

 It was on 20th of July 1888 that the man who was then known as Prince Albert Edward, but who later became King Edward VII, came to me at my lodgings in Pall Mall. He opened with the remarks, "I could of course have called on you at the Diogenes Club," he started, "but I felt it would excite too much comment. As heir to the throne, I know where the government's chief advisor lives. I have a matter of the greatest sensitivity I would wish to raise with you."

"Very good, your Highness," I replied, with as much dignity as I could muster at the unanticipated arrival of so illustrious a visitor in my unprepossessing lodgings. "What can I do for you?"

He lit a cigar and smoked it to its base without saying a word before lighting another.

"My eldest son, the Prince Albert Victor..."

"…The second in line to the throne after you?"

"The same. He has married in secret."

 I knew Prince Albert Victor was a most wild young man who left a trail of broken hearts, broken promises, and broken finances – it was only after the suppression of Albert Victor's name that I was able to allow Dr Watson to publish *The Beryl Coronet* in which a man described as being of the noblest rank but who was obviously Albert Victor appeared – but this was news to me.

"But someone in the direct line of succession such as Prince Albert Victor cannot marry without permission of the monarch, your mother. The marriage has no legal validity," said I. "It is a nullity."

There was silence and in the end I found myself posing the question.

"Who is the young lady?"

"She is a Roman Catholic prostitute called Mary Kelly."

In my position as the Government's Permanent Chief Advisor, I am used to hearing the shocking, but this was beyond anything I had heard before.

"Roman Catholic?"

"The same."

"But someone in the direct line of succession cannot marry a Roman Catholic at all."

"The matter is as I have stated."

"And she follows the way of life you say?"

"All is as I have stated."

"Who knows about this?"

"There were four witnesses – all woman following the same way of life as the bride – at the ceremony. My son has disclosed their identities to me. To my knowledge no one else knows of it and the man who conducted the service has since died."

"And how do you know about it?"

"My son told me."

"Why did he tell you?"

"Miss Kelly or Mrs Sax-Coburg as I should perhaps now call her…"

"The marriage is illegal and without validity," I reminded the prince.

"…is with child."

"And all of this he did without your permission?"

"My son is not the type to wait for me to give him permission for anything."

"But as I have already said, Your Majesty, this marriage is not legal in any sense. It does not exist at all."

"What you say is true. But if it gets out, it will be very difficult to undo without creating a public scandal."

It was impossible to disagree with this assessment. I was still running through the options in my head when the Prince added.

"And I would ask you to think of my position."

"Your position?"

"My mother celebrated her Golden Jubilee a year ago. There were plenty of protesters calling for the abolition of the monarchy alongside those who were celebrating her fifty years on the throne. Can you imagine how much greater the protests will be if something like this comes out? She is now sixty-seven and cannot go on for ever. I may not get to be king at all if knowledge of what my son has done becomes widespread."

I confess I found the Prince's focus on his own situation somewhat repellent when it was the stability of the state that was at stake, but, as I pondered matters, the gravamen of his comments was irrefutable.

Where, I mused, would the contagion stop if something like this were to become public knowledge? Would people accept Albert Victor as the heir presumptive if his association with a woman who was both a Roman Catholic and a woman of ill repute became known? And would they continue to accept the man before me, Albert Edward, and the father of Albert Victor, as the heir apparent?

Both men were, in my view, wholly unsuited to the role of monarch, but the upheaval associated with finding an alternative which would preclude either from becoming king was more than I would want to have to go through.

I considered the historical precedents.

In 1588, the Reformation, doubts over Queen Elizabeth's legitimacy, and English attacks on treasure-laden Spanish galleons had resulted in the arrival off our shores although mercifully not on them of the Spanish Armada. In 1688 doubts about the legitimacy of the son of King James II had resulted in an invasion, the king's usurpation, and the so-called Glorious Revolution.

What was it, I wondered, about years ending in eighty-eight?

And if Prince Albert Edward and his son were dubious characters, what about the presence of Albert Victor's future child. There were some who would view him or her as another claimant to the British throne, but the child's legitimacy would be even more questionable than that of Elizabeth I and the son of James II.

As I cast my intellectual net more widely and thoughts came thick and fast, the example of Prussia came to mind.

There, the man who was to become Frederick the Great and at the time heir to the incumbent King Frederick William, had had a distinctly over-familiar association with an officer called Hans Hermann von Katte. His father had his son imprisoned and forced him to watch the beheading of von Katte. I envied the power of an absolute monarch, but I realised that in a democracy like ours I would not be able to have Miss Kelly executed and the heir presumptive imprisoned and forced to watch her decapitation.

All these thoughts and more flashed through my head as I pondered.

In the end I said to the prince, "You must give me some time to consider. Pray return tomorrow when I will give you the distillation of my reflections."

My brother smoked cigarettes, cigars, and pipes when he wanted to think but for my own part I have always found snuff the best prompter of thought and I sent for three fresh tins.

The matter the prince had described I had no doubt would create a frenzy of excitement amongst all the worst informed members of British society, and even I knew not where the contagion might end. My preference has always been for my fellow-countrymen to rise to headlines about fatalities arising from earthquakes in distant countries rather than to a scandal which might cause them to call into question the institutions that have made this nation great. But, I reflected, if I were to organize a way out of this scandal I would need to identify the five women whose names I had and stage what I can only call a series of surgical strikes against them for my campaign would have to be completed without its source being traceable.

I am prepared to do anything for the smooth running of the state but even I found it hard to contemplate organizing a murder spree. It then struck me that murders were common in the east end of London and that if the man to strike the fatal blow was interested purely in murder rather than the titillations that the ladies were offering, that might make keeping wraps on it easier.

But how, I wondered, could I keep the matter quiet? As soon as I had become aware of my brother's activities and their documentation by Dr Watson, I had insisted on advanced copies of his works in case they endangered national security. This passage from what became *The Copper Beeches* now struck me as very pertinent. My brother, in an uncharacteristically insightful apercu on social conditions, opined that there, "the pressure of public opinion can do in the town what the law cannot accomplish. There is no lane so vile that the scream of a tortured child, or the thud of a drunkard's blow, does not beget sympathy and indignation among the neighbours. And the whole machinery of justice is so close that a word of complaint can set it going, and there is but a step between the crime and the dock".

In one of the places on earth most filled with vile lanes and their associated impoverished people, I was going to have to effect five killings which must not be heard by anyone. And I would have to find people who were prepared to do the work – for this was hardly a task I was myself equipped to do – and not betray what had happened. Some may ask why I did not ask my brother to do it, but my brother is an idealist to whom the idea of committing a series of murders, even if to facilitate the smooth passage of the ship of state, was unlikely to appeal. And there was Dr Watson too to consider, for he would want to make a record of events.

I decided to approach the problem from the other side and opened a second pouch of snuff from which I took a healthy pinch, and this had the effect of stimulating my intellectual capacities further.

Did I have anything at all going for me?

The killer would be briefed to kill and to withdraw. He would have no interest in the women themselves or even know who they were or why he was killing them. And no one at all would know the connection between the victims. If the killer stuck to this brief, then this would minimise the chances of him being apprehended

We could provide the killer with all the resources of the state which would mean he could be taught how to strike the deadly blow in a way that was most efficacious and most silent.

And it was here that my first really bright idea occurred to me.

 Sir William Gull was the Prince of Wales's personal physician and had taken the main role in the treatment of the Prince during an attack of typhoid fever. He had formed a close bond with the heir to the throne. I also knew that he had suffered some serious strokes which meant that while his mental alertness was unimpaired, his longevity was unlikely. A surgeon was precisely the man to show another how to kill swiftly and silently, and if that surgeon was not long for this world, he was just the man who would want to leave it in the safe knowledge that it would not change much after his death.

Another insight dawned on me. If I wanted to frustrate an investigation, it would be of considerable help if brother Sherlock was not able to become involved. I therefore determined to arrange that he be out of the country for my reign of terror.

At this point my musings were interrupted by the clang of a bell and in no more than a few seconds the Prince of Wales was once more before me. He looked somewhat put upon. "My coach driver seems to be in a rough mood even by his standards," said he grumpily. "He drove the horses from Buckingham Palace as if in a frenzy. I don't think I have ever been so knocked around in a carriage."

It was now that a masterstroke occurred to me.

We needed a killer who was invisible. Who better than a coachman?

It occurred to me that driving a carriage was how the killer in *A Study in Scarlet* had remained invisible until my brother, in a coup that I would have thought beyond his limited capabilities, realized that being the driver of a carriage lent not only invisibility but also a swift means of flight.

"Your Highness," I said, deciding in an instant that Gull and the driver of the Prince of Wales's carriage were the two accomplices that I needed, "I have formulated a plan."

 When I suggested the idea of Gull instructing the Prince's driver on a swift means to kill and for his driver then to drive his carriage around Whitechapel to carry out the necessary killings, the Prince's reaction was, "Netley is the driver's name, and he is completely mad. This would be right up his street. But," he added after a moment's

thought, "how will the coachman know where to find these women?"

I do not know how I might have answered this question if *A Study in Scarlet* had not been at the forefront of my mind. As it was, the perfect answer came straight to me for I remembered the role the Baker Street Irregulars had played in it. What was it that my brother said of them? "There's more work to be got out of one of those little beggars than out of a dozen of the Scotland Yard force. The mere sight of an official-looking person seals men's lips. These youngsters, however, go everywhere, and hear everything." A body of youngsters who could go everywhere and hear everything was just what this enterprise required.

I gave this as my answer to the Prince who sighed and said, "I am unsurprised that you have everything so well under control."

I will not weary my reader with details of how I obtained the commitment of Sir William and of Netley other than to say that Sir William commented, "I would not wish there to be any impediment to the Prince of Wales's ascent to the throne, and it would be an honour to facilitate it." For his part, Netley told me, "I picked up an infection in Whitechapel if you know what I mean. The place is full of Jews and foreigners," he added, "and I am sure it was from one of them I got it. This is my chance to get my own back."

In the end I decided that I only needed one Baker Street Irregular whom I shall call O'Wiggin, as if the son of the leader of brother Sherlock's troupe, although I will not disclose his real name as he is still alive. When I asked him to serve in my enterprise, we spent some time talking at cross purposes.

"You want me to get into a carriage with you and cruise around London, sir?" he asked. "Well, I suppose, whatever you fancy, sir. A lad like me has to make a way in life somehow and I will not be the only one in a gig like that, if you know what I mean."

He looked quite disconcerted when I told him that his role was to identify the whereabouts of women who I termed as "unfortunates" and to communicate these whereabouts to Netley.

"I am sure I could do that as well, sir, but that's not what a gentleman like you is normally looking for when he asks a lad like me into a carriage."

1888 progressed and I became increasingly confident that my plot would succeed.

I was fortunate that the early and mid-summers of 1888 saw a spate of unrelated killings of prostitutes in East London so that the first killing of my own enterprise on the 31st of August was no less than the fourth of its kind since April.

I suspect it would have attracted little attention but Netley, who from the first instructions from Gull and using swine as his practice victims, had shown a disconcerting relish in what he had been asked to do and had rent the animals' cadavers asunder.

He posed as a client, and the woman in question, Marie-Ann Nickols took him to a narrow alley-way and bent over to accommodate him. Netley gouged out her throat before she could scream using a knife of Gull's own preparation. Treating the woman's body in the same way as he had the animals he had practised on, he then dismembered her upper body, disembowelled her, and splayed her intestines over each of her shoulders.

The second killing just over a week later followed the same pattern.

Netley drove, O'Wiggin acted as his scout in and outside the carriage, and it was Netley who struck. The carriage, its windows covered with black paper, formed a convenient hiding-place – I felt that I was both present and not present as the killings, swift and silent as Netley had been instructed – took their course. I had taken the precaution of dressing myself as a police superintendent and wearing a false beard as I took the view that a man in uniform would attract few questions and little suspicion in a part of the City already filled with policemen. I went to a costumier in Paris to have the replica uniform made as I wanted to be sure it fitted my ample figure, and I felt having such a thing made abroad would attract fewer questions.

On the night of the 29th to the 30th of September we were out again.

Netley had just departed to deal with one of the women on the list when O'Wiggin returned and hissed through the darkness, "I've found another! She's less than a mile away."

"Tell Netley," replied I and in a few moments Netley was back.

"I made sure this first one was dead, sir," Netley grunted to me through the window of the carriage. And then to O'Wiggin, "Here's a bit of her apron. Have the blade of the knife clean before we get to the next one."

And then we were off.

A sudden thought struck me as we rattled along.

"What have you done with that piece of apron?" I cried to O'Wiggin.

"I chucked it away, sir," he said, sounding startled at my question.

"How often must I say we can leave no trace of who we are or where we go," replied I in some alarm.

"I'll go back," he said, and before I could say a word the coach stopped, and I heard the sound of the youth's feet land on the road as O'Wiggin disappeared into the enveloping night.

Netley whipped up the horses once more and the coach thundered through the blackness. No more than two or three minutes more and we were at Mitre Square where O'Wiggin had said one of the other women on the list was to be found.

Netley descended and I waited.

I was startled when there was a frantic banging on the side of the coach and was relieved when I heard that it was O'Wiggin.

"Sir, the police had found the apron before I got there and there is some writing on a wall above it. You had better come. It's at Goulston Street."

43

I would be a liar if I said I found following O'Wiggin on foot through London's dark alley-ways easy, but by the time we got there the crowd had still only grown to a few constables one of whom held up a lantern. In its flickering light I could see some chalk lettering on a wall, which read "The Juives are the men who will not be blamed for nothing."

I had early in the enterprise decided that the only quarter I would give to the dictates of *Realpolitik* would be that I did not want anyone to be falsely accused of the trail of killings. My superintendent's uniform enabled me to pass through the scrum of constables to the front. I knew that the writing on the wall had nothing to do with the killing, but the text would implicate the owner of the hand that wrote these words as well as stirring up anti-Jewish and anti-French feeling. Accordingly, I had the message recorded by one of the constables, who, fortuitously ignorant of French, took it down as, "The Juwes are the men who will not be blamed for nothing." I then had the message expunged. As the chalk disappeared I saw Inspector Lestrade dash up and noted the presence of the loyal but limited Dr Watson. To get away unrecognised I feigned an attack of faintness and, as I fell, I took out the lantern plunging us into darkness. In the subsequent melee escape was easy even for someone of my girth and, it hardly needs saying, even easier for the slight O'Wiggin.

As I sat over breakfast in the Diogenes on the morning of the 30th of September, I felt a mild sense of satisfaction. Four of the five women on the list that the Prince had given me no longer posed a danger to the smooth passage of the state, no one had connected the work of government with the killings, no one had been falsely charged with the killings although plenty had been arrested and freed, and, with Lestrade in charge of the case, none of this was likely to change.

The absence of my brother seemed to make the Inspector want to seek publicity so that he could be seen to be doing something. The newspapers were full of his activities. I noted he had hired two sniffer-dogs, who, the newspapers reported were called Burgho and Barnaby, to trail the killer. As the killings took place from a coach, I saw little danger from this, but I nevertheless tasked O'Wiggin to walk around Whitechapel rolling a barrel of creosote – in an overcrowded area with many trades being plied, this attracted no comment at all – which would render the dogs unable to follow any trail. The swiftness and the invisibility of the killer also inspired a lot of weak-minded would-be killers to claim responsibility and the newspapers were inundated with letters signed by "Jack the Ripper" or, "Saucy Jack". One simply signed his missive off as "From Hell". None showed any sign of knowing what was going on and, as any readers will realise, the confusion only suited my purpose.

What happened next startled even me for on the morning of the 10th of November I read in the newspaper that the fifth woman on my list had been despatched on the night of the 8th to the 9th of November. "She had her own place, so I didn't need anyone to show me where she was, and I could take my time," explained Netley to me. "I expect she worked inside because she was scared of going out on the street. So it was easy to get in." Netley did not tell me of the complete desecration of the victim's body that the extra time at his disposal gave him, but this was in any case irrelevant to the matter, and on Monday the 14th of November I was able to report to the Prince that his son's bride and the witnesses to her union with Albert Victor no longer posed a threat.

As any future readers will have seen in Dr Watson's notes, brother Sherlock had been got out of the way in Rochester near New York and I had briefed the American police to look out for attempted break-ins at the Eastman factory. As the money to finance my brother's sojourn in the United States had to come from my own pocket, I made sure that only he went. I had told Sherlock that he would have diplomatic protection for any criminal act he perpetrated but I had not told him that such protection would not be swift especially as I arranged for it not to be so. Thus it was not until the 16th of November that he was back in London to provide a briefing about the new cameras.

Although the killing of unfortunates continued throughout the autumn, the very particular method Netley had used and the subsequent gratuitous mutilation of the body were not present, and the deaths all remain unsolved.

For my own part, I was left to ponder whether it was wise to leave Albert Victor as the heir apparent and my concerns were exacerbated by his implication in a scandal at a homosexual brothel in Cleveland Street in the following year although no involvement by him was ever proved. I arranged for Albert Victor to go on a tour of duty for India in 1889 which got him out of the country. He died in an influenza epidemic in 1892. His death was thus simple to explain and, fortunately, no one sought to question why he was the only person in the royal family and its circle to be infected. I decided that there was no point doing anything to threaten the life of Albert Edward who continued on his merry way with his obesifying gluttony and his string of mistresses until he ascended to the throne as Edward VII in 1901.

He was succeeded by Albert Victor's austere brother, George, who ruled over this country and its Empire for more than a quarter of a century without a hint of scandal.

Historical Note by Henry Durham, historical advisor to *The Redacted Sherlock Holmes*

The murder spree conducted by the man who went down in legend as Jack the Ripper will be known to everyone. The details disclosed here by both Dr Watson and Mycroft Holmes tie in every particular to the events of the late summer and autumn of 1888.

What any account of the Jack the Ripper story must explain is why the killer was never caught and why the killings stopped after November 1888.

Viewed at a distance and ignoring the text above, there are two possibilities

□ The killings were random events where the killer (or killers) got lucky, and he was arrested on another charge or placed into a lunatic asylum or died before he could commit any more killings after the five.

□ The killings were carried out to order by someone whom the state wanted to protect or were carried out by the state and were of a specific list of people so, once the desired killings had been carried out, there were no more.

It seems peculiar that a killer could operate in the way that he did and not be caught.

Thus the theory that there was a state-sponsored mastermind carrying out a series of planned killings of specific people which stopped when the people on the list had been disposed of makes a lot of sense. For such a plot it is inconceivable that Mycroft

Holmes, as the mind behind all government thinking, would not have been involved.

That these accounts were penned by Mycroft Holmes himself and corroborated by a man of the reliability of Dr John Watson makes this explanation even more convincing.

The fact that it was in September 1888 that George Eastman filed his patent for rolling film in cameras is a further reason for regarding the accounts of John Watson and Mycroft Holmes as worthy of trust.

L'Affaire Dreyfus

An Account by Mycroft Holmes

Preface

In the works published in my lifetime about my younger brother and me, none pits us against each other as happens in the matter that follows.

My brother remains motivated by a love of truth and justice.

For my part I see it as my responsibility to seek political advantage for this country.

Truth and justice, while doubtless very worthy things, must sometimes take second place to the pursuit of national advantage, and, while the objectives might coincide, it is perfectly possible for them to clash as they do here.

For the benefit of those who may at some point read this work as an entertainment rather than as a treatise on statecraft, I present the matters that follow in a form which highlights this clash. Thus, what follows consists of a series of scenes documented by Doctor Watson in his somewhat romanticised style and by me in the ascetic style in which, in my view, matters ought to be retold. At the conclusion of this matter, I took all of Dr Watson's notes and embargoed their reproduction *sine die* for reasons my readers will entirely understand.

This account is thus the only true, synoptic, and, above all, complete version of events.

Part 1 by Mycroft Holmes

The Arrest

It was on the evening of Wednesday the 10th of October 1894 that I had adopted my normal station in my nook of the reading room in the Diogenes Club. I had just started my perusal of that morning's *Times* when the doorman came to me and handed me a note that read, "There is a gentleman to see you in the Stranger's Room, Mr Holmes."

I was soon shaking hands with an elegant moustached man of about the same age as me. "I am Jean Casimir-Perier," said he, "and I am President of France."

This latter remark was slightly unnecessarily as once my visitor has said his name, his role was naturally known to me.

I share my brother's facility with foreign languages and in my description of events both French and English were freely used. Accordingly, I will not mention what language was used unless relevant to the narrative development. On the rare occasions I use French in what follows it is normally because French simply provides the *mot juste*.

"And how may I help you?" I asked, curious how I, a man who has been described as *being* the British government, might help France's president.

"Your brother," said my visitor, "has described himself as the world's only consulting detective. I wonder if you might be interested in becoming the world's only consulting advisor to governments around the world – so if Grover Cleveland, President of the United States, or Leo von Caprivi, Chancellor of Germany, were at a loss as to what to do, they might come to you just as I, the president of France, am coming to you now and just as Inspector Lestrade consults with your brother."

"My work for my own country's government is its own reward," I replied cautiously. "Perhaps you could be more specific on what you have in mind."

"I have been president of France since June. I was voted in after my predecessor was assassinated by anarchists."

My interlocutor paused as though in the grip of a powerful emotion.

"Mr Holmes," he came out with at last, his eyes widened to their maximum extent, "my country is at all times on the brink of exploding. In the last hundred years we have had a revolution which resulted in the decapitation of the king, and we have had the Napoleonic Wars which resulted in the defeat of France and the occupation of Paris by foreign powers." He paused before continuing his list. "We have had the Franco-Prussian War of less than a quarter of a century ago which resulted in the loss of Alsace-Lorraine in the east of our country and the expulsion of everyone from there who did not want to take German citizenship. This was followed by a second occupation of Paris followed by a commune in Paris which had to be suppressed with great loss of blood."

"I cannot imagine, Monsieur Casimir-Perier," I replied cautiously after the President had completed this lengthy list, "that you have come here all the way from Paris with the objective of giving me a lesson in French history."

For answer, my visitor went to the window and looked out. "I see London with its calm streets and its prosperous businesses. I feel some of that would be welcome in my land."

"Two-hundred-and fifty years ago, Monsieur Casimir-Perier," I observed, "we had a civil war which also resulted in the decapitation of the king. After that we had the ousting from the throne of James II of the House of Stuarts and his replacement by a Dutch couple as part of the so-called Glorious Revolution. We have had two attempts since then by the Scots to restore the usurped Stuarts to the throne. No one would call the history of this country uneventful."

"But the events you refer to are all well over one hundred years ago."

"It is true," I conceded, "that this country has generally been at peace over the last century. I see it as my principal role to keep it that way."

"One hundred years of a land at peace! What would France not give for that?"

"Dr Watson bestows on my brother powers that are described as barely human. I fear that though my brother has been kind enough to express the view that I am his superior, it is not in my gift to bestow on your country a hundred years of peace."

There was a pause as I waited for Casimir-Perier to make his point.

"As I mentioned to you, France had a war with what is now Germany which resulted in the occupation of Paris. Although relations with the Germans have now been normalised, the tensions between our countries remain great. In September, a French spy working in the German embassy in Paris found a letter to the German military attaché which betrayed secrets of the French army."

"What secrets did it betray?"

"Some technical notes on a hydraulic brake, notes on the disposition of our cover troops, modifications to the artillery formations, and matters relating to Madagascar."

"Pray continue."

"The letter was handwritten and had been composed by someone from the French army as only someone from there would have known of the matters referred to. When the matter comes out it will cause outrage across France."

"But surely it will not come out unless you know who composed the letter as the investigation will take place in secret. Is this not a matter you should be raising with my brother?"

"We think we do know who wrote the letter."

"If you know who the traitor is, why have you come to Britain at all?"

"It is a matter of statecraft. We want to pursue the charge so that the traitor is prosecuted and punished but not so that the popular outrage causes the government to fall. There will be those who believe that the man we think is the traitor is innocent. There will be others who think he has been too leniently dealt with if he is found guilty and punished no matter how harsh that punishment is. You are the world's leading expert in statecraft, and I would like to commission you to enable us so to prosecute the traitor to bring home the charge and yet to avoid popular unrest."

"Why would a prosecution cause popular unrest?"

"There are three reasons. Firstly, we French have not yet forgiven the Germans for winning the war of twenty-five years ago and suggestions of spying by them will exacerbate tensions between our countries. Secondly, our army appears to have a traitor in its midst, and that will encourage rumours that we were betrayed in our defeat then. And thirdly, when we lost Alsace-Lorraine in the war, the population there was offered the choice of moving to France or of taking German citizenship. Many chose to leave and that meant that Paris was filled with expellees many of whom were Jewish who felt they had no future under the Germans. This meant there were fewer houses, less food, and fewer jobs to go around. That caused huge popular discontent. The man we think leaked this secret is an Alsatian Jew so this will scratch open many different old wounds."

"So you think a man whom the Germans forced to flee France as he did not want to take German citizenship is likely to want to be in German service as a spy?"

"Who knows what he might want to do? People are motivated by love, by money, or by a professional slight."

"So is your alleged spy having an affair with a German woman?"

"As far as I am aware, he is married to a French Jewess, and they have children."

"Is he in need of money?"

"It would surprise me. His family still owns businesses in the Alsace, and his wife is the daughter of a diamond merchant. As well as that of course, he has his army salary, so he is a wealthy man."

"And what has his professional progress been in the army?"

"Mr Holmes," said Casimir-Perier, I think at a loss as to how to meet my objections, "we have not commissioned you to investigate the guilt of the accused. There is no need for you to look for a motive for his crime as the evidence that he betrayed the secrets is clear. You are being commissioned to help the French state to deal with the popular reaction which will arise from the verdict. Our suspect's name is Dreyfus. He is to be confronted with his crimes on Monday. It would be good if you were there when that happened."

In 1894 I was forty-seven and still learning the art of statecraft. As my reader will discover, I had good reason to raise objections on the assumed guilt of the suspect. It was only after much soul-searching and, with the permission of authorities in this country whose names I cannot even now disclose, I agreed to go to France, and arrived there on Sunday the 14th of October. I found a note at my hotel asking me to be at the French Ministry of War on the Rue St-Dominique for a quarter to nine the following morning.

I arrived at the massive sprawling building at the appointed time and was taken to an imposing office with a desk, a table, three chairs against the back wall, and a number of alcoves two of which were curtained off. Monsieur Casmir-Perier was there with a uniformed officer who was introduced to me as Commandant du Paty. Casmir-Perier said, "We are expecting the traitor at nine. He has been told he is to face a general inspection of officers. This is a routine event, and he will only suspect something is unusual when he finds he is the only officer in the building. Your job and mine is to observe what happens from behind the alcoves in the wall, which, as you will have seen are curtained. I would beg you do nothing to give away your presence or mine. We are not to take any part in this at all. Proceedings will be organized by the Commandant here who is of a suitable rank for this role."

I did as I was bidden, and just before nine o'clock, I could see through a tiny crack in the curtains what I presumed to be three witnesses join du Paty in the room. On the dot of nine there was a discreet knock on the door and a small, bespectacled man presented himself.

Du Paty opened proceedings.

"I have a letter to write to my superior and I have injured my hand," he said in a plaintive voice to Dreyfus. "Are you able to write to my dictation?"

I think Dreyfus was surprised by this request, but he agreed, and du Paty started his dictation.

Paris, 15th of October 1894

Having the most serious reasons, Sir, for retaking possession of the documents I passed to you before taking off on manoeuvres, I beseech you to have them brought to me immediately by the bearer of this letter who is to be trusted.

I recall for your benefit that this is a matter of:

1 °) A note on the hydraulic brake of 120 and the way in which this part behaved.

2 °) A note on the cover troops (The modifications will be made by the new plan).

3 °) A note on a modification to the artillery formations

4 °) A note relating to Madagascar.

Le Paty interrupted his dictation.

"Dreyfus, you are trembling."

"The outside air was cold, Commander, and I fear I have not yet warmed up."

At this point, du Paty put his hand on Dreyfus' shoulder and announced in a voice of thunder, "In the name of the law I arrest you on the charge of high treason."

He took a pistol into his hand and pointed it at Dreyfus who slowly raised his hands. He then handed Dreyfus another pistol.

"There is a single bullet in this pistol I am giving you," said du Paty to Dreyfus. "You may use it if you want to make things easy for yourself."

There was a pause.

Was Dreyfus going to kill himself before us, I speculated?

"You may kill me if you wish to, Commander. I will not kill myself," came a steady voice.

"That is not a job for us, Dreyfus."

"Then there is nothing to say. I have done nothing of which I am ashamed, and I will not kill myself to make your life easy."

"Then you are under arrest and court martial proceedings will follow."

"Very well. Then let them commence."

There were no more than a few moments of further discussions and then Dreyfus was marched from the room.

Part 2 by Dr John Watson

The Trial

1894, the year of Holmes's return from the dead, was a busy one.

In my account of *The Norwood Builder* of that year, I refer also to the case of the papers of Ex-President Murillo, and also the shocking affair of the Dutch steamship Friesland, which so nearly cost us both our lives although Holmes, perhaps expecting a faster restart of activities after his three-year absence, found the months after his return uneventful.

It was on Friday the 14th of December that we returned to Baker Street after a ramble though London when the boy in buttons informed Holmes, "Two gentlemen to see you, Mr Holmes. Didn't catch their names. They spoke foreign."

We were halfway up the familiar seventeen steps, when Holmes stopped, a look of excitement in his eyes. "Two Frenchman are awaiting us behind the door," said he.

"How do you know?"

"Dear Watson, does your nose not pick up the acrid smell of black tobacco? In our room our visitors are smoking cigarettes from France. The smell of an Englishman's cigarette, by contrast, carries the mellowness of its fine Virginia tobacco. To the expert nose, it is like the difference between a rousing espresso and a soothing cup of tea."

Our visitors rose from their seats as we entered.

One, tall and slim, was a man in his early forties with a well-maintained handlebar moustache. He rose from the fireside as we entered and extended his hand. "I call myself Mathieu Dreyfus," he said in an accent which sounded, as my friend had predicted, French, although I felt that there with a hint of something else in it.

"I note you are here from France," observed my friend, "yet Dreyfus does not sound to my ears a very French name."

It soon became obvious that Dreyfus's command of English was limited while my friend's grasp of the language, as I have set out elsewhere, was sufficient for him to quote Victor Hugo in the original and my knowledge was sufficient to understand him when he did so. We thus soon switched to French although I will continue to recount what was said in English.

"I am a Jew," said Mathieu Dreyfus, "and from the Alsace which used to belong to France, but which has been annexed by the Germans since the war of 1871, so my family and I were forced to flee. The Dreyfus name is a common one among Jews and comes from the time when Jews were forced to take family names in Austria. Some were able to take pleasant names such as Schönberg which means Fair Hill or Weissblum which means White Flower. And some were forced to take names such as Grünspan which means verdigris or, as in my family's case, Dreifuss."

"What is verdigris?" I asked, having never heard the word.

"It is the green deposit which forms on unpolished copper. Dreifuss, which was the original form of my name, means three foot and so is equally unattractive. When we were forced to move from what had become Germany, we dropped the second 's' to make the name sound more French. "

Our visitor paused and lit another cigarette before he continued.

"But I have not come here to discuss the derivation of my name. A major miscarriage of justice is taking place in France, and I would like the help of Mr Holmes on it. This man here," he went on, with a wave at his colleague, a sober looking figure with long sideburns, "is Monsieur Edgar Demange. He is the legal counsel for the defence in the case."

"Very good, gentlemen," said Holmes, "perhaps you would like to give me some details."

"My brother is a captain in the French army. He has been arrested on charges of spying for the Germans."

"What is the basis of the charge?"

"You will understand, Mr Holmes, that I can only tell you what I have been told myself by my brother who is the accused. A section of a letter which has come to be known as a bordereau – which may be translated as a deposition – was discovered by a French agent in the waste-paper basket of the German military attaché at the German embassy in Paris. I do not have the document or a copy of it, but I do know its contents were as follows.

Our visitor handed my friend a piece of paper on which had been typed the following:

"Without any news that you want to see me, I would like to send you some interesting information, however.

1 °) A note on the hydraulic brake of 120 and the way in which this part behaved.

2 °) A note on the cover troops (The modifications will be made by the new plan).

3 °) A note on a modification to the artillery formations

4 °) A note relating to Madagascar.

5) The draft field artillery manual (March 14, 1894).

This last document is extremely difficult to obtain, and I can only have it at my disposal for a few days. The War Ministry sent a fixed number to the relevant corps, and each corps is responsible for them. Each holding officer must hand over his own after the manoeuvres. So, if you want to take what interests you and keep it at my disposal afterwards, I will take it. Unless you want me to copy it in full and send you a copy.

I am going to go on manoeuvres….

"A dangerous but by no means definitively treasonous document," commented my friend. "It betrays a willingness to pass secrets, but it is not clear that any actual secrets have been passed. And this can only be an extract of a larger document. And is the link to your brother established?"

"As you say, this document is an extract of a larger document, and it is undated. My brother had not recently been and was not intended to go on manoeuvres before he was arrested. The officers of the French army spend most of their time living in their own homes in Paris."

"And does he have any knowledge of the matters referred to?"

For the first time our visitor looked a little uncertain of himself.

"My brother in in the Artillery so he would know about the first and third of the matters. But," a fierce look came over Mathieu Dreyfus's face, "he has never been to Madagascar, and he knows nothing about it."

"But he might have found something out that was written by someone else that is not public knowledge and that may be of use to the Germans."

"I concede that that might be so," said Mathieu Dreyfus reluctantly.

"Everything that Monsieur Holmes is saying makes sense," broke in Demange. "That Monsieur Holmes is able to take a broad view of the evidence will help us in this matter."

"Has your brother need of money?"

"Even though we were expelled from the Alsace, we have retained our business interests there. And my brother's wife is the daughter of a diamond merchant. As well as that he has his army salary."

"But he may have major outgoings for matters he has not told you about."

"None that I am aware of, and he gave me no reason to think he was being extravagant in other areas."

"So how has this document been associated with your brother?"

"The original document was handwritten. The handwriting of the original document is said to match that of my brother."

"And does it?"

"My brother's court-martial is due to be held next week and writing experts will pronounce their views on it then. One of them is the famous scientist Alphonse Bertillon."

The name Bertillon caused my friend to start.

"Ah, good Watson, do you remember how Dr Mortimer at the time of *The Hound of the Baskervilles* compared my scientific methods to those of Monsieur Bertillon. My recollection of events is that the comparison was to my disadvantage."

"And my recollection of events is that you were not a little put out by Doctor Mortimer's verdict," I replied cautiously, as I knew how easily Holmes felt slighted.

"At last, at last I may have the opportunity to test my powers against his," said Holmes ignoring my response. He turned to our visitors. "And what do you want me to do?"

"Mr Holmes," said Demange, "last year your colleague Dr Watson published a work called *The Reigate Squires,* in which you made observations about two people who were partners in a murder based on a few handwritten words found on a tiny scrap of paper in the grasp of the victim."

"If you can do so much with so little, Monsieur Holmes," broke in Mathieu Dreyfus earnestly, "I am sure that you can do even more for my brother who remains in prison."

I could see how the prospect of preventing a miscarriage of justice appealed to my friend as his eyes were as if lit. He grasped my arm and said, "Watson, it is a question of honour. We have no choice but to go to Paris."

"You understand our visit may serve only to confirm the guilt of Alfred Dreyfus," I objected.

"I would regard even a clear answer on the culpability of my brother as a result," said Mathieu Dreyfus, rather to my surprise. He sounded a little wearied as he continued. "It is difficult to live with the uncertainty. It took several days before we even found out my brother had been arrested when he disappeared in October. At least if his fate is decided clearly, his wife and his wider family can move on. For my own part I have no doubts as to his innocence."

"The charges against my client," said Edgar Demange, "are based on a single piece of evidence. It is the handwriting on the letter which is said to be a match for his."

"And is it?"

"I do not know. I will not see it until we are in court next week. We have only heard the matter would come to trial yesterday and we came straight here. We have very little time to prepare. I would like you, Monsieur Holmes, to be the member of the defence team who questions Monsieur Bertillon."

"Am I allowed to do that in a French court?"

"Monsieur Holmes, this is a military court, so the normal procedural laws of France do not apply. I have already cleared your presence with the presiding judge and the prosecution."

"They know my identity?"

"As I said, this is a military court, and the judge can accept any procedure he likes. He has accepted that you will be part of the defence team, Monsieur Holmes."

Holmes spent the next few days updating himself on the case in French newspapers.

"France seems torn asunder," said he to me at one point. "In this country newspapers would not be allowed to speculate on the guilt of the accused. In France the papers seem to discuss nothing else unless they are dedicating their energies to discussing whether the trial should be held in private or in public. Those who want it to be held in private fear revealing secrets to the Germans. Those who want it held in public say that only a public trial will lance the boil of treachery. There is almost but not complete unanimity on Dreyfus's guilt."

"And what is your view?"

"It is hard to see how a fair trial, whether public or private, can be held at all when everyone seems convinced of the guilt of the accused and hard for me to form my own view as well. Everything seems to be based on the handwriting of one deposition and its apparent match to Dreyfus's writing. We are heading into choppy waters."

It was in a sombre mood that Holmes and I crossed a turbid English Channel, and the cold grey afternoon of Wednesday the 19th of December 1894 found us in the forbidding prison of Cherche-Midi in the heart of Paris. The building had been planned as a military prison and so had a large but austere room which could be used as a judicial court. Before proceedings began Holmes was given half an hour to familiarise himself with the evidence. After that, we went into court where it was standing room only as it had been decided that the public should indeed be admitted.

The fair, pince-nez wearing Alfred Dreyfus, much slighter than his brother and with a pencil moustache in sharp contrast to his brother's handle-bar, entered and was allowed by the presiding judge, Colonel Maurel – one of seven judges for the case – to be seated. The charges were read out and the Captain pleaded not guilty.

The prosecuting counsel, Monsieur Brisset, gave a summary of the prosecution's case. "I will show to the court," he said, "that I have a hand-written document which betrays the secrets of the French army. I will further demonstrate that this hand-written document is from the hand of the man before us, Captain Dreyfus."

Brisset then summoned his star witness, as expected, Alphonse Bertillon.

"I am," began Bertillon with an air of authority, "an expert in all aspects of human physiognomy. I was brought this bordereau," – Bertillon flourished aloft a piece of paper, "in October. It contains a treasonous offer to reveal state secrets to the Germans. I conducted research to find out who had written it, and I found an exact match with the hand of the prisoner. You will see from the loops of the 'l' and the accuracy with which the dots of the 'i' are placed over that letter, that it could only come from the writer of this document," here Bertillon flourished another piece of paper, "which was penned by the prisoner at dictation before his arrest."

I expected Bertillon to continue but instead he sat down and said, "I have said all that I intend to say, gentlemen, and I rest my case."

Holmes rose.

"Monsieur Bertillon, could you tell the court your qualifications to pronounce on handwriting."

"I am a scientist and an anthropometrist, Monsieur Holmes."

At this point I saw a note being passed to Maurel.

"Can you explain to the court what an anthropometrist is?" asked Holmes.

The chief judge interrupted proceedings.

"If there is to be forensic questioning of witnesses, we cannot do this in open court. It risks giving an outsider too much insight into the operations of the army. There will be a break of fifteen minutes while the court is cleared of the public."

The court room was much more comfortable a quarter of an hour later when only people with a direct connection with the case – I was admitted as part of the defence team – were present.

"So, Monsieur Bertillon," continued Holmes when the proceedings had started up again, "you were about to explain the work of an anthropometrist."

"I measure parts of the body and their proportions to one another. I arrive at conclusions which are used to provide forensic evidence for police investigations. I have also pioneered the use of galvanoplastic compounds to preserve footprints, written studies on ballistics, and introduced the dynamometer to determine the degree of force used in breaking and entering. I noted, Monsieur Holmes, that you made use of some of my techniques in your monograph on footprint preservation which you, in your own words, admitted to being guilty of – rather like the prisoner although he has not confessed his guilt."

"Monsieur Bertillon, it is your testimony that is being tested here and not my monograph. May I ask if examination of handwriting forms any part of your normal activities as you have not mentioned it in what you have just said?"

"Not…. specifically."

"So, in your work for the police, have you ever done analysis of handwriting?"

"No."

"And yet you are certain that you can identify the writing of the bordereau and of Captain Dreyfus?"

"My work is focused on the little things. They are infinitely the most important. I think it was you who originally said that."

"You say in your comparison of the two sets of handwriting that the 'l' is looped in the same way in both specimens and that the dot over the 'i' is placed with the same precision."

"That is so."

"But if you look at the vertical proportions of the letters," Holmes showed the court the bordereau and the text Dreyfus had written to dictation, "you will see that the upwards and lower extensions are much more pronounced in the bordereau."

A shrug.

"And," continued Holmes, "the small 'b' is open at the top in the bordereau but closed in the sample of Captain Dreyfus's writing."

There was a long pause and Bertillon shrugged again.

"I expect Monsieur Dreyfus was attempting to disguise his writing in both versions of text   both the bordereau so that no one could see his hand behind it, and the text he took down to dictation when he realised he was reproducing the bordereau text. In those circumstances one must expect some inconsistencies."

"But you would say the two sets of writing are written by the same hand in spite of these inconsistencies."

I expected a reasoned response from Bertillon to Holmes's questioning. Instead Bertillon pointed theatrically at a cross on the wall.

"Mr Holmes," he cried, "I can swear by that crucifix that the prisoner here before us is guilty of treason. And he?..." Bertillon swung round to point at Dreyfus, "he cannot similarly swear his innocence. I have nothing further to say and will now leave the witness stand."

Numerous other witnesses were called. Other experts in handwriting gave conflicting views but none with the drama or passion of Bertillon. Character witnesses for Dreyfus were also called and gave what felt to me to be rather lukewarm endorsements. By Saturday the 22nd of December, all the evidence had been submitted.

Holmes and I were asked to the home of Mathieu Dreyfus, and we waited for the telephone to ring with the verdict. The call came at half past seven. We were unsurprised that it was a guilty verdict, and a second call told us that Captain Dreyfus had been sentenced to life imprisonment. "They cannot condemn him to death as the death penalty has been abolished for political crimes. My brother will be exiled to Devil's Island off the coast of South America. And that will amount to a capital sentence as no one can be expected to survive long in a place like that," said Mathieu. "And they are going to cashier him," he continued, "which will involve a process of *la dégradation*."

There was a pause and then Dreyfus said, "The fight to clear my brother starts now but I cannot expect you gentlemen to stay in France for that. I would like to thank you for all you have done."

Part 3 by Mycroft Holmes

The President and the Verdict

I spent the evening awaiting the verdict with the French President at his Champs-Élysées Palace having spent the previous three days in court hidden in an alcove just as I had been when Dreyfus was arrested. I was in reflective mood as no one had forewarned me that my brother would be part of the defence team.

My original advice had been to hold the trial in public to clear any doubts in the mind of the public of the prisoner's guilt, as long as the evidence was conclusive, which I had been told it was. As soon as I realised young Sherlock was on the defence team, I knew the evidence must be more dubious than had been indicated to me and that it would be examined by someone who had at least a limited grasp of how it should be called into question.

Heated discussion amongst the French population on whether a guilty verdict was the correct one did not seem to me to be helpful to the President if he wanted a land at peace for the next hundred years. Consequently, even after the passage of many years, I regard my decision to pass a note to the main judge asking him to make proceedings private as something of a masterstroke. Star witness Monsieur Bertillon's evidence was questionable at best, and the less of it that got out into the public domain, the better. Dr Watson above has not covered the rest of the proceedings, but they were in my view equally unsatisfactory in demonstrating the guilt of Dreyfus.

I suppose on balance that a guilty verdict was better for the President than one which left the passer of secrets to the Germans unidentified, and he certainly seemed to think so.

"A triumph!" he exclaimed, and he embraced me, something which my readers will be unsurprised to learn was not a common experience in my life. "And now we must make the most of it!"

"What are you going to do?"

"We must let popular rage be satisfied so that we can move on. In the very old days we would have tied his limbs to horses, and they would have been flogged to try to tear him apart. A hundred years ago we would have made do with the guillotine. Now we must satisfy ourselves with *dégradation*."

"What is that?"

"You will see, my friend."

I was uneasy with this familiarity but let it pass. "We stopped public executions in Great Britain because the desired effect of making punishment visible was offset by our inability to control the crowds," I said in the end.

Casimir-Perier shrugged. "I will have every soldier in Paris at the parade ground where *la dégradation* passes itself so the crowd will not – how do you say? – lynch Dreyfus. You may come along if you wish to be present."

"I fear," I said, "that I do not see the purpose of that. You must do with your verdict as you see best. It will be very hard to resile from it if you do what you describe."

Casimir-Perier shrugged again and that was the end of our exchange.

Part 4 by Dr John Watson

The Investigation

There seemed nothing more to say and a day and half later saw Holmes and me back at Baker Street.

As my readers may imagine, Christmas in Baker Street passed almost unrecognised – the only thing to reveal the special date was the dearth of callers to Holmes. Some Christmases this dearth lightened my colleague's mood, "I suppose I should not begrudge it that on this day even the felon is not engaged in his employment," he had said at one previous Yuletide, "although it does make my life rather dull." But in this year of 1894 Holmes was as preoccupied as I have ever seen him. He smoked one cigarette after another and strode the length of the little sitting room sometimes addressing me and sometimes himself. "Not only was the evidence that was presented flawed, but Alfred Dreyfus had money in his own family, a wealthy wife, and salary as a captain. He had no need to sell secrets. Yet now after the guilty verdict there will be no movement on this unless we can find out who really wrote that bordereau."

As well as reading the British press with his customary avidity, he ordered in the French newspaper and scoured them too

– I could see that the press wrote about nothing else apart from *L'affaire Dreyfus*.

One morning just after Christmas he suddenly said, "But of course! Much the likeliest thing is that whoever did betray the secrets was motivated by money. Well, there is an easy way to check that out."

"How will you do that?" I asked somewhat sceptically.

"We will break into the payroll department of the French army at the army headquarters at Vincennes east of Paris."

"But there are hundreds of thousands of soldiers in the French army. Even if you can get in, you will not be able to spend long enough in there to read all their records. And Vincennes is an ancient military fortress."

"But I will only be looking at the records of soldiers who have had advances on their pay as that will indicate financial stress. And there will be two of us looking. And this coming weekend there is the *dégradation* of Dreyfus at the French military school in the centre of Paris, so Vincennes is likely to be deserted as every soldier in France can muster will be sent there to control the crowds. The early morning of Saturday will be the perfect day to break in."

I confess were it not for the fact that I felt a grave injustice had been committed, I would not have countenanced becoming involved in anything like this. As it was, my disquiet about the verdict on Dreyfus and Holmes's enthusiasm for his ideas won me over completely.

"You are right Holmes," I said, "we are bound to go."

"I knew you would not fail me at this moment," replied he, and was moved enough to wrap me in an embrace.

We got to Paris on Friday the 4th of January and it was still dark when we got to Vincennes in the city's eastern suburbs on the following morning. Readers may share the scepticism I had initially felt about how easy it might be to break into the French army's headquarters but *The Bruce-Partington Plans* and *The Naval Treaty* both reveal the ease with which important documents could be abstracted from British government buildings by intruders. A combination of Holmes's skills, a diamond tipped glass cutter wielded under a dark lantern, and some sloppy work by the very few guards on site, soon demonstrated that French buildings were no more secure than their British counterparts. Holmes, who had been reading everything he could about the medieval fort and how it had developed, found his way to the payroll department as though he was a clerk who worked there every day.

"We are not looking at individual files at this stage, Watson," he said, effortlessly opening the filing cabinets with a skeleton key and running his forefinger down a long list of soldier's names, "but at the monthly payment lists. They will show gross amounts and deductions. So tax, mess bills, and what we are looking for: repayments of advances."

We soon detected a population of about fifty soldiers who were paying back advances on salary and one name immediately caught Holmes's eye. "Look at this Watson!" he exclaimed, "this man Charles Ferdinand Walsin Esterhazy is paying back almost as much in advances as he is earning in salary. And," he added, looking back though other payroll listings, "it is happening month after month. Each time one advance is paid back, he takes out another."

"Walsin Esterhazy does not sound a very French name," I remarked.

"Walsin sounds German and Esterhazy Hungarian. Esterhazy was the name of the prince who employed the composer Joseph Haydn at his court and had lands across Europe. It is an aristocratic family of great fame and wealth, but this man appears not to share in the wealth, or he has a grossly extravagant lifestyle."

Holmes then used his skeleton keys once more to open some other filing cabinets until he ran down the personnel records of Walsin Esterhazy.

He opened the folder, and his breath came out in a hiss.

"Look at the writing on this letter, Watson. It is asking for an advance. And the dots exactly placed over the 'i', there are the same loops in the 'l' as on the bordereau. But also the same open formation of 'b' and the same upper and lower extensions. And look Watson, here is the man's address in 12 Rue St-Étienne. He is forty-seven years old. We have him, good Watson, we have him!"

He paused for a second and then gave a little dance of triumph before adding, "By Jove, it is well thought!"

He went over to one of the clerk's desks and picked up a piece of headed note paper and an envelope. He then sat down and wrote a short note. He put it into the envelope, addressed it, and tucked it into an inside pocket.

"And now back to the hotel," said my friend.

As we headed to the centre of Paris, Holmes said not a word. He bought some stamps at the reception of the hotel, and asked.

"Is the post collected on a Saturday?"

"Yes it is, but it will not be delivered even within Paris until Monday morning at the earliest," said the receptionist.

We went to the post-box and Holmes put his letter into it. "Not even that master blackmailer, Charles Augustus Milverton could have done it any better," he said, as we heard the soft thud of the letter landing inside.

As we went back to our hotel, Holmes picked up an evening newspaper with the headline "Enfin la dégradation", - Enfin means at last, and my readers will need no translation of "dégradation" once they have read the text below.

The article beneath the headline ran as follows:

"Today saw the cashiering of the man everyone in the country wants to see hanged.

Dreyfus sold national secrets to the Germans and now he was humiliated before the nation which had given him refuge and which he has betrayed.

One minute the traitor stood in full uniform on the parade ground of the École Militaire with his ceremonial sword in its scabbard. The next the sword had been seized and broken in two and all the emblems on his uniform had been ripped off. He stood there almost naked and all the while protesting feebly but unconvincingly in his Germanised French, "I am innocent! Vive la France! I am innocent! Vive la France!"

The baying crowd was not to be fooled by Dreyfus's words and, though held back from tearing him apart by barriers and line upon line of brave French soldiers, they cried, "Death to the traitor! Death to the Jew!"

These cries were still ringing out when Dreyfus, now fittingly degraded, was packed into a carriage, and taken back to prison. He will now be transported to Devil's Island off the coast of South America where his remaining life is likely to be nasty, brutish, and, if there is a God, short."

"And what are our plans now?" I asked, sobered by the treatment of a man who was innocent of a crime which Holmes had now proved to have been committed by someone else.

"We can do nothing till Monday, but we must be ready at the Rue St-Étienne at first light then. I will go and reconnoitre there tomorrow and on Monday you must have all your travel documents and your pistol at the ready. I have no idea where we will spend Monday night, and we may as well leave our belongings at the hotel."

On the Monday morning Holmes hailed a fiacre and hired it for the day. "You must do whatever I say," he said to the driver as he handed him a fat fee.

We drove to what I could see was a street with blocks of flats on both sides. We parked a little way down the street from number 12 and at half-past-seven the postman came and put mail into most of the letter boxes at the front of the house. Various residents came out to collect their mail.

At a quarter-past-eight Holmes nudged me as an elaborately moustached middle-aged man in army uniform came down the stairs and opened a mail- box.

"That, I fancy is our man."

The man whom I shall now call Walsin Esterhazy went back inside the building. A few minutes later, he came back out again now dressed in a great-coat and with a travel bag over his shoulder but with no sign of a moustache. He walked down the street away from us and towards the end of the road which ran into one of Paris's main throughfares.

"This looks like flight. Driver, please go to the corner," and, as Walsin Esterhazy hailed a fiacre, he added, "please follow that cab, although I assume it will go to the Gare de l'Est."

"Our quarry is going to flee to Germany and that is where most of the trains to Germany go from," Holmes added turning to me.

"What is your plan?" I asked wondering where all this was leading.

"I do not believe," said Holmes, "that if I point out to the French authorities the similarities between Walsin Esterhazy's writing and that of the bordereau that that will be sufficient to get Dreyfus released. If Walsin Esterhazy is truly going to Germany, then there will be customs formalities at what is, even nearly a quarter of a century, a closely guarded border. I will hold him up there and there will be police on hand to arrest him. They may regard his flight as evidence of his guilt, and I may even force a confession out of him."

"Why is he fleeing?"

"The note I sent him on army headed note paper said, 'Traître, votre écriture a été reconnue'. It means. 'Traitor, your handwriting has been recognised'."

Holmes lit a cigar and the end glowed scarlet in triumph before a look of concern came over his face as he noted the direction the fiacre in front was taking us. "Where are we going? We are at the Gare du Nord not the Gare de l'Est. Trains from here go to Calais and the low countries, not to Germany." Holmes's cigar continued to glow scarlet but this time the glow betokened consternation.

We followed Walsin Esterhazy at a short distance and were only two behind him in the queue for tickets. He ordered a one-way ticket to London. Holmes's face changed from concern to bewilderment at this, but we already had tickets to London and so left the queue. We followed Walsin Esterhazy as he went to the telegraph office but soon came out and we followed our suspect to the train, taking seats in the department next to him.

I will not detain my readers with an account of our journey across northern France and the Channel to Victoria other than to say that we made sure we knew where Walsin Esterhazy was at all times. It was dark when we arrived at London and from Victoria the object of our pursuit walked north-east along Victoria Street, past the Houses of Parliament and up along Whitehall, left past Nelson's Column at Trafalgar Square, and left again into Pall Mall. "But here there are only clubs and residential buildings," said Holmes to me. "What would he be doing here?...And he is standing outside the building where Mycroft's flat is – just opposite the Diogenes Club."

Suddenly a familiar voice from came from across the road. "Major Walsin Esterhazy! I was watching my flat from my club opposite and saw you arrive and wait outside as we agreed by telegram. And I suppose I should not be all that surprised to find my brother and the faithful Dr Watson trailing behind you. I am not allowed to have three guests at once in the Diogenes, so you had better come into my flat. There is only seating for one so you three gentlemen will have to stand."

I have referred elsewhere to the "little sitting room" at Baker Street.

Mycroft's bare sitting room was a lot smaller. Walsin Esterhazy stood in a corner while Holmes and I stood with our backs to the window. We all looked enviously at Mycroft Holmes sat in an armchair by the fireplace for it was a cold night.

"So Major," said Mycroft, "you feel your safety is in danger as your penning of the bordereau has been uncovered. You fear the fate of the unfortunate Captain Dreyfus being visited on you."

The major confined himself to a nod.

"I had hoped, dear Sherlock, that you would not uncover my little scheme. I am in the process of organizing the negotiation of what I suspect will be known as the *Entente Cordiale* with the French which is basically an agreement for confirming that we will be aligned with them should another German/French conflict arise. Of course we are also, in parallel, negotiating the *Traité d'Amitié* or the Treaty of Friendship with the Germans, although French is the language of diplomacy and that is what gives the treaty its name, with the grand-son of our queen, Germany's Kaiser Wilhelm. This second treaty also states with whom we shall be allied in the event of such a conflict although the counterparty is not the same that envisaged in the *Entente Cordiale*."

I have elsewhere categorised my friend's understanding of politics as zero and it was I who responded, "So you are negotiating treaties with both the French and the Germans at the same time, and each has the opposite effect of the other?"

"It is called diplomacy, dear doctor, and obviously we will dump one treaty party when the time is ripe to sign a treaty with the other. It could be at any time and with either party. Or not at all."

"So what does Major Walsin Esterhazy have to do with this?"

"It is necessary to keep both sides on the hop. If they are not mutually suspicious, they may see it as in their interests to form an alliance against us instead. For this reason, I have paid our friend the major here to abstract French secrets and pass them to the Germans just as in Berlin I have a man – who, for reasons you will understand, I will not name – passing German secrets to the French."

Mycroft's daring and his utter lack of scruples quite took my breath away, but it was Holmes who raised the first objection to this scheming.

"And Dreyfus has been made to face a trial, been found guilty of a charge of which he was innocent, degraded, and is about to be sent to Devil's Island because of your machinations."

"I rather fear that there are some matters that must be regarded as collateral damage, dear brother."

85

"This is not 'some matters'. This is a person who will probably die soon as I imagine Devil's Island will have got its name for a reason. Do you have a plan to right this wrong?"

"What about me?" broke in Walsin Esterhazy. "I have been risking my life for your machinations and now I have nothing."

"As to you, Monsieur Walsin Esterhazy," countered Mycroft, "you have no cause for complaint. You have been handsomely rewarded for your part in my schemes as well as receiving money from the Germans. And you have your army salary."

"I have spent almost all that I received and all the assets I have in France are valueless as I cannot now go back there."

"I do not believe the French authorities will find out that you are the man behind the betrayal of secrets and, given the lengths they have gone to say that Dreyfus was the culprit, they will be most unlikely to want to declare that they have got it wrong even if they do discover who the real author of the bordereau was."

"You cannot guarantee that," Walsin Esterhazy wheedled. "I saw what happened to Dreyfus. I would not wish that that happened to me."

"Very well, I suppose it will not be too difficult to find another person in France to do the same thing as you have done, maybe even at a lower price. We will find a place for you in this country to go into exile."

"What about Dreyfus?" insisted Holmes.

"For the reasons I have just indicated to the major, I do not think there will be any appetite among the French authorities to reopen this matter. The only evidence is based on handwriting, and we have already seen how divided opinions can be on that. I will look to see if I can do anything about it if it happens to be with the French we eventually choose to ally ourselves. If we should choose to ally ourselves with the Germans or with no one at all, I fear I am unlikely to be able to intercede."

Part 5 by Mycroft Holmes

Reflections

I suppose individuals should matter in the grand scheme of things – but not as much as the serene process of the British state towards the sunlit uplands.

My own preference was for what I regarded as the process towards the signing of the *Entente Cordiale* and what others, somewhat dramatically, referred to as the Dreyfus Affair, to fade away but in 1898, the writer Émile Zola, produced an inflammatory pamphlet called *J'accuse* which cast doubt on the original verdict.

Dreyfus was retried but reconvicted and I felt unable to do anything about it. I decided in the end that Britain's best interests would indeed be best served by the *Entente Cordiale*, and this was eventually signed in 1904. Once this was done I was able to advise the French of the miscarriage of justice that had occurred.

Dreyfus was released in 1906 and went back into the army where he continues to serve. In the Great War just passed he rose to the rank of Lieutenant Colonel.

I was able to agree with the British Prime Minister that we should offer Walsin Esterhazy the status of a refugee and he was settled in the blameless town of Harpenden, north of London. He was continually short of money just as he had been when he was selling secrets and in the end he redeemed his financial fortunes by offering the noble Esterhazy family that he would stop using their name as his in exchange for a financial settlement.

Within a few days of the passing of the verdict, Casimir-Perier stood down as President to be replaced by Félix Faure. Casimir-Perier had been a businessman before he became President and returned to that.

Émile Zola, who wrote the pamphlet *J'accuse,* which called into question the verdict on Dreyfus, died in a mysterious accident in 1902 when the chimney of his bedroom was blocked by builders working on the house next door and he was asphyxiated. Zola was originally buried in the Cimetière de Montmartre in Paris but was reburied in the Panthéon in 1908. By the time of the reburial, Dreyfus had been freed and attended the ceremony at which there was a failed attempt on his life.

For reasons my readers will understand, I cannot regard my attempt to make France a land of peace with itself a success.

I had complex material to work with and the presence among my adversaries of my coltish but not unintelligent younger brother complicated matters further.

At a distance of several decades, I confess that I feel the brief would have taxed greater minds than mine should any such minds exist.

Historical Note by Henry Durham, historical advisor to *The Redacted Sherlock Holmes* series

The discovery that the true betrayer of French military secrets was in the pay of Mycroft Holmes resolves many of the mysteries of the Dreyfus Affair.

French historians (Jean Doise, Michel de Lombarès and Henri Giscard d'Estaing), though differing in the details of their theories, are united in their puzzlement at the innocuous nature of what was passed to the Germans. Among the bits of information that the writer of the bordereau offered to pass to the Germans, Madagascar off the east African coast was of no interest to them as their colonial activities were in south-western Africa and the French Army had already rejected the 120 mm model of the field-gun as unworkable and had begun development 75 mm version. It is noticeable that the Germans did not even bother to dispose of the bordereau securely perhaps indicating the lack of importance they attached to it.

That Walsin Esterhazy was being used by Mycroft as a means of disrupting Franco-German relations thus makes a lot of sense, and the finding of these notes are a major step forward in resolving this still controversial mystery.

Some Taxing Matters

Preface by Henry Durham, historical advisor to *The Redacted Sherlock Holmes* series

What Mycroft Holmes relates below refers to matters that arose between 1926 and 1934 and is precise in the sums of money involved.

Readers may wonder what these sums are worth in twenty-first century money.

This preface was written in 2025.

Readers are safe to multiply numbers below by fifty and to convert sterling amounts into United States dollars at a rate of USD 4 to the pound to get the value in 2025 money.

Thus £1,000 in 1930 is worth USD 200,000 in today's money.

Some Taxing Matters as narrated by Mycroft Holmes

In Dr Watson's accounts of my brother's activities most of the people who consulted him came from the ranks of the lowlier classes – a tide-waiter, a woman letting out a spare room, a lovelorn typist, a railway porter in a velveteen uniform. By contrast, all the people who visited me at my humble apartment in the Mall or at the Diogenes Club were from the highest echelons of society – indeed I have yet to feature a petitioner in my own writings who has not attracted a string of biographers.

The matter I relate now tells of one of the great politicians of the twentieth century and of one of its great writers.

My brother has commented that part of my regimen was to be at the Diogenes Club which is just opposite my bachelor apartment from a quarter to five until twenty to eight in the evening. It seems hardly worth mentioning that a man of my class would not prepare his own breakfast, so another part of my regimen was to be at the Diogenes at ten past eight in the morning for the first meal of the day where I stayed until nine o'clock when I departed for Whitehall. It was when I arrived at the Diogenes for breakfast on the 12th of February of 1926 that the doorman approached me.

"There's a visitor waiting for you in the Stranger's Room, sir," he said. "He has been waiting for you for ten minutes and has already asked me to bring him a large glass of whisky and soda which I will have to add to your account."

As my readers will know, the Stranger's Room overlooks Pall Mall.

I went into it to find one of the best-known figures in the country sitting at the window and looking down over the street below.

Mr Winston Churchill was puffing a large cigar and had already half-drained his glass. All the pictures ever shown of Mr Churchill have him, besides the inevitable cigar, wearing a bow tie and a waistcoat with a gold watch chain across it. This accorded precisely with how he was dressed now. At this stage of his career, he had already been President of the Board of Trade, Home Secretary, First Lord of the Admiralty, and Secretary of State for the Colonies. Now he was Chancellor of the Exchequer, and so the man in charge of the nation's money.

As the British Government's Permanent Chief Advisor, I had of course worked with Mr Churchill on numerous occasions. During the Great War I had rather thought that he would be this country's next Prime Minister but three, but he had blotted his copybook most notably in the Dardanelles Campaign of 1915/1916, and his elevation to that lofty office had had to wait. His unorthodoxy – going as Home Secretary to the Sidney Street Siege to observe police activities there, inventing the tank, being associated with the army putting down a miners' strike in South Wales – meant that he was regarded with suspicion by many.

"How can I help you, Mr Churchill?" I asked as he turned to face me.

"It is a curious thing," he started.

I waited to hear what he would say next, and in the end he went on, but what followed seemed to be the Chancellor talking to himself although he addressed me.

"When I was Secretary of State for the Colonies in 1922," he said at last, "I had to have an appendectomy. While I was recovering, an election was held, the vote went against me, and I changed political allegiance. So it was that I found myself without an office of state, without a seat in Parliament, without a party to represent, and without an appendix to do whatever an appendix does. And yet I have always given fully of myself, and, truly, I deserve all the political popularity I can get."

Mr Churchill came to a pause, drained his glass, and then tapped the hanging ash of his cigar stub into a club ashtray which already had sufficient ash in it to suggest that he had smoked two cigars before the one he was now extinguishing.

"I thirst," he commented, apropos of nothing in particular.

"Only members can buy drinks here," I objected.

"If you could then be so kind, perhaps this time asking your barman to give a slightly greater emphasis to the spirit and slightly lesser emphasis to the soda."

I was not sure how to respond to this – I had a pension but saw no reason why I should subsidise what I shall cautiously call the thirst of a politician who had a much higher income than I had. In the end I felt I had not been left with any choice, so I summoned a waiter and asked him to add another whisky and soda for Mr Churchill to my account.

"The matter is this," said Mr Churchill at last. "As a government minister, I am banned from making money apart from the rather miserable salary I am allotted for my service in office."

"Your earnings as Chancellor of the Exchequer are a matter of public record and you are on £4,000 a year (*Note by Henry Durham*: so, in line with the note at the head of this text, USD 16,000 per annum or USD 800,000 in 2025 money)," I objected. "I am reluctant to comment on my own financial situation but in 1895, Dr Watson, in one of his many prolix and frothy romances, disclosed my earnings to be £450 a year. That was over thirty years ago but even in these times when inflation has debauched the value of our currency, that only equates to £900 per annum so you earn more than four times more than I did when I was at the peak of my earning power and when I was described as *being* the British Government."

"Regardless of your income, how wealthy you are depends on your outgoings," rejoindered Mr Churchill. "I assume you still have bachelor headquarters here in Pall Mall and remain a regular attendee here…"

I nodded.

"I, by contrast, have five children who must be suitably educated. Besides that, I have a love of travel, of the gambling-table, and of painting. I enjoy fine cigars, champagne, and whisky and the adjective I have used applies to all three of these life essentials. As well as all that, I have a political career to sustain and several properties to maintain. My regular outgoings are twice the salary I receive as the highest paid minister in the Cabinet after the Prime Minister."

"These outgoings, if I may say so, Mr Churchill, are discretionary expenditure. You are not obliged to incur any of them. They are not wholly, necessarily, and exclusively" – I knew that these three tests were the ones any outgoing had to pass for it to be allowable for tax – "incurred for the furtherance of your trade."

"That is so," conceded Churchill. "But when I am not in the office of minister, I can work as a journalist to supplement my income. I am highly prolific in that capacity, and it is highly remunerative. It is when I am in office that my income is not sufficient to cover my outgoings. So it is that my chosen career path reduces me to penury when I have achieved its goal of being in office."

"You are obviously using some definition of penury I was not previously aware of," I objected. "Your salary as Chancellor places you comfortably in the top one per cent of earners in the country."

"Yes, but my outgoings, if I may make so bold, are off the scale compared to anyone else in the country and my salary, by comparison, is chickenfeed."

I was not sure where this was leading. I was concerned that Mr Churchill's remarks may be a prelude to him leaving public office and I felt that the nation had a use for a man of his talents.

"So when you are not in office, how do you fund your lifestyle if you cannot write?" I asked at last.

"I speculate in shares."

"Profitably?"

"I play the tables at Monte Carlo."

"Profitably?"

"I have, as you say, my writing," said Mr Churchill, suddenly sounding slightly grumpy. "My books have a huge popular following – much as the books of Dr Watson have – and my articles are fought over by every major newspaper in this country and abroad. I cannot now write but I do receive royalties for works I have produced in the past."

I noted that Mr Churchill had made no comment at all on whether his speculations at the gambling tables or shares made a profit. And I made no attempt to get involved with him on any discussion of Dr Watson's works which constitute one of those rare matters on which my brother's opinion and mine are closely aligned.

"What is it you want me to do, Mr Churchill?"

"I have a £3,000 tax bill shortly falling due on the profits on my writings. If I am to be candid, I have no means of paying it. I am at the limit of my overdraft and all my assets are under a heavy mortgage. When Dr Roylott in *The Speckled Band* found himself in this situation, he took to trying to murder his stepchildren by having a swamp-adder, the deadliest snake in India, bite them, so that the income intended for them would come to him. I would not go as far as doing that, but I need you to find a way of making the Inland Revenue take a sensible view of my liability."

"When you say, 'taking a sensible view', you mean you want me to find a way for you to avoid paying the tax?"

"You put it more bluntly than I would."

"But that is the substance of it."

"Yes."

"And you would not wish anyone else to be able to use whatever method you adopt."

"My situation is all my own," this said with an unwavering stare. "No one else courts the approval of the general public as I do."

"And this general public you refer to – you would not wish it to be aware of your tax avoidance?"

"It would be difficult to persuade this general public to pay its taxes if it is known that the man responsible for imposing those taxes was not himself paying them."

"So, if I may sum up Mr Churchill, you want your avoidance method to be unique to you so that no one else can use it, private from everyone else so that it does not damage your political reputation, and effective so that you end up paying nothing."

There was a pause, and I added, "And you want me to find a way to do this in the face of legislation devised by the top lawyers in the land to prevent precisely that."

There was now a long pause as Mr Churchill considered what was in my view a very simple and precise summary of what he was looking for.

"Yes," he grated out at last. "That is what I want you to achieve for me."

And with that Mr Churchill polished off the rest of his drink in one gulp, puffed on his latest cigar so that the tip glowed red, ground it out with a quite disproportionate ferocity in the ashtray which was now full to overflowing, and was gone.

I repaired to breakfast, grateful that being surrounded by fellow members of the Diogenes Club would mean that no one would pay the least attention to me while I ate it, and I would thus be left in peace with my contemplations.

I had concluded it would be desirable if Mr Churchill continued as one of his country's representatives and there was a danger that he would leave public life if he was not able to earn enough to pay for his preferred life-style. How, I mused, could one man, no matter how lofty the office he held, escape the clutches of a body as all-seeing, faceless, and demanding as His Majesty's collector of taxes, the Inland Revenue? The whole point of laws, I mused – whether of tax or of anything else – is that they do not admit to personal exceptions.

And yet, as I reflected, while organizations, countries, and empires may have the characteristics I have referred to, they also have leaders and their representatives, and those leaders and representatives are human beings, and human beings are wont to be attracted by baubles. My readers may wonder if that remark might apply to me in my capacity as the British Government's Permanent Advisor, but I would draw their attention to the work Dr Watson published as *The Bruce-Partington Plans* where my young brother said of me, "(Mycroft) remains a subordinate, he has no ambitions of any kind and will receive neither honour nor title, but he remains the most indispensable man in the country."

Any intervention on my part, I decided, would have to be made at the level of someone who made decisions and yet felt undervalued.

It was in the work by Dr Watson referred to above that my brother referred to me as *being* the British Government. By 1927 my status was perhaps less the Government's Advisor and more its Advisor Emeritus, but I knew enough to know that the Chairman of the Inland Revenue, the government's tax collection service, was called Richard Hopkins. He was a man still in his mid-forties, but he had already been a Civil Servant for twenty years. What might be the next move he might want to make and how might I enable it? And what might he wish to avoid?

I gave the matter further thought. If Hopkins gave Churchill some sort of exemption from paying the taxes due, he would probably not want to be around to face any later consequences. How would the Government's Treasury be as his next potential move?

I knew the Permanent Secretary to the Treasury – such an absurd title, it made one of the most senior civil servants in the country sound like one of those lovelorn typists that so litter Dr Watson's works – was a man called Sir Warren Fisher, and the beginning of his service coincided with the last years of my own. Would Fisher have in his department a position which Mr Hopkins might aspire to?

Before I made my way to the Treasury I went to a stationers and bought some high-quality note paper. Quite contrary to my normal literary instincts, if that is the right term for what I deploy when I write, I will at this point keep my readers in suspense as to what I did with this paper other than to say that I penned three short documents, one a simple announcement, one muted but incendiary, and one merely incendiary but not intended for circulation of any sort.

The name Mycroft Holmes meant I had an entrée to every government department, and I was soon before the glossy-haired and suave Sir Warren at his desk in the Treasury.

"Do you feel," I asked him, apropos of nothing in particular, "that you progress?"

"I feel," replied Sir Warren thoughtfully, "that I could do more in the service of my country although it is always a matter of opportunity and resource."

"What might enable you to do more?" I persisted.

"An extra brain. Though for what I do, I would want a brain that was honed but not honed quite as well as mine. I would not, if I am candid, wish to have someone working in my department who might challenge my own progression."

"How about 'Hoppy' Hopkins at the Inland Revenue?"

"He seems to me steady and suitably unambitious," said Fisher after a moment's reflection.

"Would the position of your deputy in the Treasury attract a knighthood?"

"I am sure it might be made to do so."

"Do you have anything to say against him?"

"It is his job to be in a position where he attracts no attention in any way, and he has never done so. He is, if I may make so bold, a safe pair of hands. As a civil servant you are always afraid your name will be on the front of a newspaper, but it is politicians who take the limelight and the blame, and that is what they are paid to do. A civil servant grinds away in the background, does all the work, and gets none of glory. A politician does none of the work, but he gains all the credit – although, obviously, he does also get the opprobrium if things go wrong."

"How might that apply to a tax-collector?"

"In the position of a man who is responsible for collecting the nation's taxes, a newspaper can always claim that the collection rate is too low and too slow, or indeed too harsh and repressive. But it would normally be the Chancellor of the Exchequer to whom the head of the Inland Revenue is responsible who would carry the can for any error of omission or commission."

"But he may seek to lay any problem at the door of one of his civil servants."

"That would be most... unorthodox..." Sir Warren's voice trailed away.

Having secured Hopkins his next move upwards, I repaired to the Inland Revenue's offices a few doors down Whitehall and was soon before the tall, serious, bespectacled Mr Richard Hopkins.

"I was of course fully aware," said he in welcome, "that the great Mr Sherlock Holmes had an elder brother who *was* the British government. But I advisedly use a past tense, and I had no idea he still carried out government business or that I would have the honour of having him here before me."

"I am here on a mission," I said without preamble. "Mrs Maud Radcliffe of Epping is being harried by your inspectors for death duties following the departure from this life of her husband."

A look of some alarm came across Mr Hopkins's face. "But that is not a matter for me. If she has a complaint she cannot resolve with one of my tax officials, she should raise it with her Member of Parliament, who is her representative. If she lives in Epping that will be…"

He broke off as it occurred to him that the member of Parliament for Epping was Mr Winston Churchill, Chancellor of the Exchequer, and the man to whom Hopkins was ultimately responsible.

"The Chancellor is unorthodox…most unorthodox," said Hopkins in a faraway voice. "I assume that he wants to lay this at my door and that of my inspectors."

"He is well-connected to the newspapers," I commented airily, "although he does not write for them at present as he is in office. It would be unfortunate indeed if your name were to appear in them. And I expect that advances in photography would mean that your picture would appear on the front page of every newspaper in the country which may not be what you wish." I left a pause before I continued. "You might be referred to as 'Hopkins, the widow-harrier'. That would be a pithy and alliterative headline which might appeal to an enterprising journalist."

I left another pause before continuing.

"If that were to happen, it might be felt that your judgement is not perhaps quite…. sound. You may need to be transferred to another position within the Civil Service. Perhaps the Ministry of Agriculture may need to someone to specify the amount of land to be given over to the cultivation of the mangold wurzel. Securing sufficient feed for cattle is crucial for the feeding of the country and is a task well suited to your skills in numeracy as you use your slide-rule to find the optimal use of agricultural land."

I am sure Hopkins had not been anticipating any of this, and I went on.

"Like Mrs Radcliffe, Mr Churchill is also struggling with his tax bill. He has a liability of £3,000 which is being chased up by your inspectors with the same alarming alacrity with which they are chasing up Mrs Radcliffe's liabilities."

Hopkins's face fell further but, finally, he spoke.

"Are you really saying that the Chancellor of the Exchequer is looking to me to obtain a personalised dispensation to enable him to avoid tax which is due under the law?"

"This is clearly not a matter that he would wish to progress on his own behalf. I confess I have really come here, Mr Hopkins, to have a philosophical discussion with you about the nature of income."

"The nature of income?" ejaculated Hopkins, perplexion written across his features.

"Mr Churchill is planning to retire as an author as he is too busy being Chancellor of the Exchequer to do any writing at present. The Chancellorship is a post which he plans to occupy for some time."

"Pray continue," said Hopkins, I flatter myself unsure as to where this was leading and so completely lacking the self-assurance that my brother would have displayed had he said these words which were such favourites of his.

"As he is retiring, he feels that it would be appropriate if the puny sums he gets from his writing via his publisher…"

"…His tax liability is £3,000," interrupted Hopkins. "The sums involved can hardly be said to be puny. On the contrary, they bespeak a large income if the income tax liability is so large …"

"…could be treated as capital receipts paid to him by the public, rather than as income. The money he has received could be seen as being advanced by the public to him with the publishing companies merely serving as the conduit through which the money is channelled. A receipt of capital is not a source of income and so is not liable to tax."

"But every author in the country could claim that."

"But not every author in the country is Winston Churchill. And not every author is planning to retire. And not every author is Chancellor of the Exchequer and the man in charge of the organization that you work for," this last remark delivered with a look straight into Hopkins's eye which caused him to squirm in his seat and avert his gaze.

"What do you want?" he asked after a long pause and looking slightly dazed.

"Your agreement in writing to what I have proposed."

There was a long pause and then came the question – delivered in a half-strangled voice while Hopkins focused his gaze on some particularly fascinating aspect of his shoe – that I had been wating for.

"What is in this for me?"

"We feel, Mr Hopkins, that you have been long in this office and the country would benefit if you had a new challenge. The Permanent Secretary to the Treasury is looking for a new deputy. This position comes with a knighthood although I am sure the baubles of recognition would not sway your judgement in any way."

The great master of statecraft, Niccolò Machiavelli speculated in *Il Principe*, normally somewhat loosely translated into English under the title *The Prince*, on whether it is better for a ruler to be loved or feared. He inclined towards the latter.

Somewhat contrary to the ideas of the Florentine master – the only person with whom I would wish to be compared – I feel that it is better still if one is both loved and feared. At this moment I certainly felt that plain Mr Richard Hopkins both loved and feared me. I was in the happy position of having him by a sensitive part of his anatomy and, as is the way with such things, his heart and mind soon followed. And yet the prospect of a knighthood was being dangled before him. He was, I mused, both in fear of his appearance on the front page of the newspapers and filled with pride at the prospect of becoming Sir rather than merely Mr Richard Hopkins.

It was a while before the mixture of emotions cleared from his face but, eventually, the visage of a man committed to doing his professional duties returned.

"What do I do next?"

I was ready for this too.

"I prepared this letter earlier in the day," said I, putting a piece of paper down in front of him. "If you could transcribe what I have written, we can make sure Mr Churchill gets it by the end of the day. The matter will be closed, and you can start in your new role tomorrow."

"I would like confirmation of my knighthood in writing from you now."

"Here too I can help. It is not for nothing that I have been described as *being* the British Government and I have that confirmation here. You will be on the honours list to be published in June," said I and put down another piece of note paper with the full announcement.

I have always thought that with a reluctant counterparty a stick is valuable as well as a carrot and with a flourish I put down the third piece of paper and added, "And here is the relevant article for the *Daily Express*. This is what will be published tomorrow if you do not comply. I have not included your home address in the article, but you will understand that this is a detail any journalist worth his salt can look up in these new-fangled telephone directories."

A pause, and then Hopkins asked, "Do you want my advice to Mr Churchill on Inland Revenue headed note-paper?"

"I think it is better if it did not bear the imprimatur of the Inland Revenue as then we would need to keep a copy of it on our records. I have brought some blank notepaper with me."

"Do you want me to get it typed?"

"I think it would be better if it were in your own hand. It is far harder to forge or deny the authenticity of a full-length handwritten document than a document typed by someone else and then signed by you. I fear I cannot spare the time to look at the quality of typed lettering as my brother did in *A Case of Identity* to prove a document's source."

"Very well."

Before my eyes Hopkins sat at his desk and transcribed what I had written:

Dear Mr Churchill

As I understand the matter, you feel yourself precluded by the responsibilities of your office as Chancellor from continuing to exercise the profession of author or indeed to write for profit in any way and you intend merely to complete certain minor outstanding engagements already entered into before joining the Government. Upon the assumption that before the end of this tax year, the 5th of April 1926, you have completed any outstanding contracts and received payment therefor, and thus cease definitively as an author, it is my judgement that you will not be liable to pay tax for your work as an author and any future earnings from your existing writings will be seen as gifts from the public and so also not liable to tax.

You may refer to this letter in any future correspondence with the Inland Revenue although you may find that any official you deal with is already appraised of its import.

I remain, your obedient servant,

Richard Hopkins

"Truly," said Hopkins with a sigh as he handed over the letter, "we apply the law to everyone, but we interpret it for our friends."

"It is always good," responded I smoothly, as I checked what he had written to ensure that there were no departures from my text, "to have officials in government who can see both sides of any argument."

And with that I returned to the Diogenes.

My readers may think that the matters I relate have reached their conclusion but in fact there is still quite a long way to run.

In 1934 I arrived once more at the Diogenes Club to be advised that a visitor was waiting for me in the Stranger's Room. I entered to find myself confronted by another figure who will be well known to my readers. PG Wodehouse's smoking preference was for a pipe, and he sat where Mr Churchill had sat eight years before. The humourist – creator of Jeeves, Bertie Wooster, Mr Mulliner, and Psmith – sat enveloped in the mellow smoke of his pipe and sipped at what smelled to me like Darjeeling. In spite of his soothing choices in both tobacco and beverage, Mr Wodehouse looked, if not exactly disgruntled, certainly far from being gruntled.

"I have," he said in gentle low voice, "a small problem with which I need some help."

"I hear many problems," I replied, "but few, alas, where my skills are of much use."

"As a writer, I have few outgoings. I can claim a small allowance for my house, I can claim for the cost of a typewriter and of paper. Apart from this the royalties I earn are fully chargeable to tax which on the top slice of my income runs at ninety-seven and a half per cent of my earnings."

Mr Wodehouse looked at me with the air of someone who had drunk the cup of life and found a beetle at the bottom of it as he said these words.

For my part I reflected, fortified by my experiences with Mr Churchill, on how I might help Mr Wodehouse and decided to put some questions to him.

"How many books do you write each year?" I asked.

"Four on average. A mixture of novels and short story collections, generally twelve short stories to a collection. I write for the stage as well."

I confess I had had no inkling of Mr Wodehouse's industriousness, which put even the prolific Dr Watson into the shade.

"And have you given any thoughts to abandoning your writing now that you have already written so many works?"

"I was once in banking. That is why I am now in writing."

"And how much is your writing worth to you?"

"One hundred thousand pounds."

"No, it is your annual earnings I am interested in," I replied, "not your career earnings."

"One hundred thousand pounds is the amount I earn each year from my writing," replied Wodehouse (*Note by Henry Durham*: so, in line with the note at the head of this text, USD 400,000 per annum or USD 20 million in 2025 money). He puffed at his pipe so that the smoke swirled up and he seemed surrounded by mist.

I confess I had not followed Mr Wodehouse's activities with sufficient closeness to have formed a view on what he might be earning, but even I, who is used to hearing the most outlandish things, was taken aback by this figure.

I felt constrained to say, "But that is twenty-five times more than what the Chancellor of the Exchequer earns."

"And on the great majority of it, the same Chancellor you refer to takes ninety-seven and a half per cent or nineteen shillings and sixpence out of every pound. I am as broke as the Ten Commandments were after Moses had returned from his first jaunt up Mount Sinai to commune with the Almighty."

"How long," I ventured, "do you intend to go on writing?"

"Our conversation has thus far been brief," replied Wodehouse, "but, I would like to think, unambiguous and I would refer you to my previous remarks. I will carry on writing until I think of something else I can do. I first wrote an article I was paid for thirty years ago, and no alternative has occurred to me since. I fear I shall go like a performing flea pretty much until I drop."

"Have you given any thought of moving abroad?"

"I spend much time in the United States – so much so that the American authorities have also taken an interest in me. Like the British tax authorities, they have an approach to exacting taxation not unlike that of putting a lemon into a vice and turning the handle. If I were a pip of the said lemon, my squeaks would be deafening."

I mused what I could do to help Mr Wodehouse. I could see no role he could play in the furtherance of this country's ambitions, I could see no argument that he was going to stop earning the outrageous though legal sums he was making, and I could see no great advantage to the country if Mr Wodehouse remained in it, especially as he already seemed to spend a lot of his time overseas.

"I fear I can think of nothing that will help you. The country cannot make an exception for one of its writers to avoid paying tax. If it makes an exception for you, then there would be a queue of other writers."

My interlocutor is noted for his observation that a ray of sunshine and a Scotsman with a grievance are seldom confused and there was no doubt that it was the latter which Mr Wodehouse now more closely resembled. He continued puffing at his pipe. In the end I left him to his musings and went to breakfast.

Maybe it was I who planted the seed in his head but shortly afterwards I read that Mr Wodehouse had moved to Le Touquet in France. The French authorities had given him a special dispensation so that he did not have to pay the level of taxes that would normally fall due on his earnings – something it is much easier for a foreign government to provide to a British writer than it was for a British government to do as once one has made one exception it is hard to avoid making more. Mr Wodehouse was slow to flee France when the Germans attacked that country in 1940, and I cannot but wonder whether fears about his tax situation if he returned to this country made Wodehouse tardy to take flight. Whatever the motivation, his tardiness means he is now in German custody.

But the events I relate above were not an end of the tax problems of Mr Churchill. He had fallen from office in 1929 and subsequently, not to put too fine a point on it, "unretired" as a writer.

He produced a four-volume life of his ancestor, the Duke of Marlborough, went on lecture tours in the United States, wrote extensively in the press at home and abroad about the gathering storm engulfing Europe and, by my judgement, earned comfortably enough, even after tax, to pay for his extravagant life-style. It is extraordinary to realise that this was to become once more unsustainable when he became Prime Minister in 1940 even though he then earned a quarter more than he had done as Chancellor of the Exchequer. The war meant he was now unable to go to Monte Carlo and wager a fortune in the casino, but his tax liabilities threatened to engulf him once more, and he sought my counsel as he had no other means of earning a living other than as Prime Minister.

I agreed to pay a visit to the by now ennobled Richard Hopkins on the Prime Minister's behalf. He had risen not only to the position of Permanent Secretary to the Treasury but also to that of Head of the Civil Service. It was a pleasure to be able to see him and not have to resort to blackmail and bribery to help Mr Churchill escape tax on his past earnings as a writer by the same mechanism as he had used in 1927 – indeed, I can report that Sir Richard agreed to my petition on behalf of the Prime Minister with the single scribbled word, "Acquiesce" thus obviating the need for me to provide a suitable text for him to put his name to.

I write these lines in my nineties and in my eighth decade of service to the Government. I continue to watch Mr Churchill and his appetites with some wonder. In the war we find ourselves in, with most of the things he cherishes either closed or in short supply, he rushes round the world, his energies undiminished. At some point he will cease to be Prime Minister. It is hard to imagine him not wanting to unretire for a second time to earn some income and subsequently to retire for a third time to protect that income from tax.

Historical Note by Henry Durham, historical advisor to
***The Redacted Sherlock Holmes* series**

Research into the tax affairs of Winston Churchill and PG Wodehouse confirm the historical accuracy of the foregoing.

The prediction made here by Mycroft Holmes that at some future point Churchill would unretire for a second time and then re-retire for a third time also proved accurate.

The expression that, "Only little people pay taxes," is attributed to Leona Roberts Helmsley (1920 –2007).

The account set down here by Mycroft Holmes would appear to lend support to this observation.

A Case of Paternity by Dr John Watson

It was the summer of 1935.

Although my eightieth birthday lay behind me, I was still running a practice in Queen Anne Street. It was a beautiful day, and I was listening to a patient, a Mr Gladwyn, talking about his problems with flatus. These problems were very current and assailed more than one of my senses. For most patients and most complaints, I recommended changes to the complainant's regimen of tobacco and alcohol consumption, but I could not see that this would be relevant here and I found myself, quite at variance to my normal modus operandi, making suggestions about diet and recommending a course of charcoal biscuits.

Suddenly the door opened, and Mycroft Holmes walked in. He was as massive as ever and his grey eyes had all the mastery which I have previously described to readers of my works.

"I have a matter of state I would wish to discuss with you, Doctor," said he. He turned to Mr Gladwyn. "This matter outweighs in importance anything you might be discussing with the Doctor."

It is hard to muster an argument against the masterfulness of Mycroft Holmes, and I said to my patient, "I think we had all but finished Mr Gladwyn."

Once Mycroft (whom I shall normally refer to as such to avoid confusion with his brother, Sherlock) and I were alone, Mycroft spoke about the reason for his visit.

"We will soon be joined," said he, "by a Herr Felchner from Berlin who works as a civil servant in Germany's air ministry. Herr Felchner has telegrammed to say that he has a matter to present which if left unchecked poses a danger to the German Reich."

"I am trying to run a medical practice here," I grunted, slightly nettled by Mycroft's apparent assumption that I would drop everything at his unannounced arrival for what seemed the vaguest of petitions.

"I note you are a little engaged at present, but if you are concerned about neglecting the needs of your patients, I am happy to be able to tell you that I have brought my young second cousin, Dr Verner, along with me. You will recall it was he who bought your practice at Kensington after my brother's return from the Reichenbach Falls in 1894. He has now retired but would be happy to step in as your locum."

In no more than a few minutes, Verner was seated behind my desk and listening to another patient who was, coincidentally, also troubled by flatus. Mycroft and I withdrew to the private part of my house, and we were soon joined by Herr Felchner. I was surprised that a civil servant at the German air-ministry in Berlin wore a dark blue uniform. I was even more surprised when he clicked his heels, raised his right arm, and cried "Heil Hitler!", circling to take in both of us in as he gave his salutation.

I had no idea how to respond to this and even Mycroft, as unperturbable a man as it was possible to imagine, seemed nonplussed.

I have referred in the works I have published in my lifetime to the linguistic abilities of Sherlock Holmes, but I have never referenced Mycroft's abilities in this area. As my readers might expect, he was at least as gifted in this respect as his brother Sherlock. I too have enough knowledge of the German language that Sherlock Holmes was able to quote Goethe to me in the original. Thus, the discussions that followed took place in a mixture of German and English as did all the numerous discussions with German officials in the account of events that follows.

It was Mycroft who opened proceedings.

"Herr Felchner has travelled overnight from Berlin to London. Perhaps Herr Felchner you might like to present to us the matter you would wish to discuss."

"I am an under-secretary at the air-ministry, gentlemen, and I report to the State Secretary who is a man called Erhard Milch. He in turn reports to the minister, the Reichsmarschall or Marshal of the German Reich, Hermann Göring."

There was a pause, and I wondered what sort of petition was coming next, but Felchner evidently felt he was only at the introductory phase of presenting what he had to say. A sudden light came into his eyes as he continued. "My country is finally on the rise after its betrayal at Versailles." He paused for a second and a look of wonder across his face. "It is truly a miracle what is happening. Although, of course," he insisted, suddenly becoming business-like, "we in Germany have no designs on any of the interests of the great British Empire. Indeed, our Führer, Herr Adolf Hitler, has always expressed admiration at how a country with a relatively small population can have assembled an empire the like of which the world has never seen before."

"Any attempt by the Germans or anyone else to build an empire of its own will necessarily compete with the British Empire," observed Mycroft mildly.

"We in Germany have no desire to build an Empire outside Europe. We wish to do no more than restore our standing within Europe where your country has no vital interests," came back Felchner earnestly. "It was in Europe that we were betrayed. We lost a seventh of our territory and our Austrian-Hungarian allies were reduced to being two rump states as Poland, Romania, and Czechoslovakia were carved out of our ancestral lands."

"I think Poles, Romanians, the Czechs, and the Slovaks were the principal occupants of the lands that now have become three separate nations, and independence was something that the majority of their citizens wanted," countered Mycroft.

I do not think Felchner had been expecting a reasoned response to his remarks and there was a pause. In the end Felchner continued, "In Germany, the Communists stopped the workers working, the Jews, who had infiltrated the Communists, served their own degeneracy, and the Catholics are more interested in their religion rather than the race. We were surrounded by traitors in every quarter."

"Does that long list of internal enemies you have mentioned not mean that those who wanted to go along with the political strategy of your country's leaders were actually in a minority?" asked Mycroft mildly.

Felchner paused to consider my friend's reaction to his remarks which I am sure he was not making the for first time but which, I am equally sure, he was used to making without contradiction.

In the end he said, "That was then. We are now no longer a democracy so who forms a majority and who a minority no longer matters. My country's political strategy was not properly communicated to the people which is why our state broke down. But now we have the Führer to lead us whereas before the Jews subverted the political will for their own interests. Once our people understand our political strategy, they will embrace it. And the Jews will be....." he broke off as though not sure what to say next.

"I follow events in Germany closely," countered Mycroft. "My civil servants tell me that the population of Germany is sixty million people of whom fewer than three-hundred thousand are Jews. How can so few people subvert a people two hundred times greater in number?"

"You do not know the Jews. Our Führer says they are a parasite in the body of other peoples. They are a nation within a nation and have an influence vastly disproportionate to their number."

"So, in other words, you despise them for their degeneracy and fear them for their ability to subvert your state. Is that not holding two beliefs at once that are mutually exclusive?"

I do not think Felchner had been anticipating a forensic analysis of his country's political direction, and he lapsed into silence.

"There are obviously some details in the Führer's thesis that still need to be worked out," he mumbled in the end.

"In this country," continued Mycroft serenely, "you will find Jews represented in every section of our society. My brother, as Dr Watson here has related, bought a Stradivarius violin from a Jewish pedlar in the Tottenham Court Road. The malefactors in *The Stockbroker's Clerk* were described by my brother's petitioner, as having the touch of what he called the Sheeny about them – a term for a Jew which I am not at all sure one would be allowed to use today when one has learned to be careful about one's mode of expression. And in my early days as the Government's Principal Permanent Advisor, I dealt with Benjamin Disraeli – the clue to his racial background is the name – who was Prime Minister of this country twice."

There was a long pause.

It was Mycroft who broke the silence and continued. "And yet the world continues to spin on its axis. And this country remains the most powerful on earth."

"Andere Länder, andere Sitten," mumbled Felchner under his breath, I think slightly taken aback by Mycroft's exegesis.

"Herr Felchner means, 'Other countries, other customs,'" translated Mycroft for my benefit while out petitioner sat apparently wresting with an intense internal struggle. He turned back to our visitor. "I think it would be as well, Herr Felchner, if you now made the point that brought you here."

"I have good reason to believe that my superior, Herr Erhard Milch, is a Jew. Our laws state that it is illegal that he should be in the employ of the German state if this is so. All Jews were dismissed from state employment as soon as our government took power for they formed their own nation within the Reich and, as I have indicated previously, served their own interests rather than those of the Reich."

I could not imagine where this was going and nor, it seemed, did Mycroft for he asked with a mild note of asperity in his voice, "What it is you want from us, Herr Felchner?"

"I would like a man of substance and with experience of statecraft – no one else fits the bill as well as you, the famed Mycroft Holmes – to come to Germany and investigate Milch's background. If you would be so kind as to confirm my suspicion, I will denounce Herr Milch to the Reichsmarschall, and the traitor will be marched from the ministry building forthwith."

The disconcerting light in his eyes that we had seen previously came back into them. "Truly he and his race are my country's misfortune."

As is the way with so many petitions I relate in these accounts of cases hitherto redacted from the record, this one was quite beyond anything I had ever heard before. I confess our client's mode of expression made me question his complete sanity. I glanced at Mycroft wondering how he would respond and noted his face still wore a look of complete equanimity.

In the end it was Mycroft Holmes who spoke and said, "May I first ask, Herr Felchner, what you know about this man Milch?"

"He is from Friedrichshafen which is a few miles to the west of Hamburg. He had a career running what are known as airlines – so companies that own a fleet of 'planes and fly people around – in the eastern part of the Reich."

"So he would appear well suited to a senior position in your air-ministry."

"My concerns are not about his suitability for his current role but about his ancestry. If my suspicions about his ancestry are correct, he will be out to...."

"Thank you, Herr Felchner," broke in Mycroft, "you have given us some useful facts. You must leave resolving your suspicions to us. We will revert to you if we decide to investigate your case."

Felchner took his leave.

I confess that I found the idea of investigating whether a man had Jewish ancestry repugnant and was unable to suppress my revulsion.

"Why," I burst out, "would this country wish to enable a German investigation born of pure racialism?"

"It is," replied Mycroft, perhaps a little loftily, "purely a matter of *Realpolitik*, which is the principal I adopt when instructing – apologies – advising our Prime Ministers. There are some who feel that it is in this country's interests that Germany should be permanently hobbled by political discord..."

"And what is your own view? How can we bring peace unto the nations of Europe?" I interrupted, curious as to what form this country's foreign policy might take.

"..Au contraire, Dr Watson," soothed Mycroft, "I think that it is in the interests of this country that political discord should hobble the statecraft of all our continental neighbours. If they are unable to plot a proper political course, there will exist between them a sense of quiet mistrust which will leave this country free to pursue its own much greater interests on the world stage. I would add that both elements of this quiet mistrust are important. The quiet will stop wars breaking out between the countries in which we may need to become involved. And the mistrust will stop alliances against us developing between the continental powers that might threaten our interests."

"Does the Great War of less than twenty years ago, with its millions of casualties, not give you cause to question this policy?" I asked.

"It is behind us, dear doctor, and my statecraft continues unimpeded," replied Mycroft dismissively. "And in spite of it, this country remains the world's greatest power."

"What is your plan?" I asked not sure how to respond to Mycroft's ruminations.

"To act, good Doctor. We will go to Friedrichshafen or wherever the trail should take us and find out whether there is any truth in Felchner's suspicions. If Felchner's suspicions are true, we can see if we can turn Milch to work for us. If Felchner's suspicions are false, we will see whether we can use Felchner to sow discord in the German air ministry as I am sure there are other people about whom similar accusations could be made."

"And, of course," I added, "if Felchner's accusations are false, it means the justice will have been served as Milch will be able to keep his position."

"It is always useful, dear doctor," said Mycroft soothingly, "to have the moral arguments represented in discussions on statecraft. I shall telegram Herr Felchner and advise him that we will act."

I will not detain my reader with details of the travel arrangements made, but two days later saw Mycroft and me at the Registry of Births and Deaths in Friedrichshafen where, to my surprise, there was a queue to enter the office of the Registrar.

Mycroft had disclosed no *modus operandi* to me so I had no idea of what would happen when we presented ourselves to Herr Klein, the elderly senior registrar, who spoke a slow but steady English.

"I am called Brady," said Mycroft to Klein in an unwonted soft southern Irish accent. "I am a lawyer from Ireland and this," he said turning to me, "is my assistant Mr Riordan." I confined myself to nodding. "I am looking for descendants of Arthur Milligan, a wealthy Irish landowner. Arthur Milligan has just died intestate at a great age. We know that his son Henry came to Germany in 1880 to work at the port here in Friedrichshafen and that he adopted the name Heinrich Milch."

"Milch means 'milk'" commented Klein, "so it may be that it was one of the first German words Milligan learnt when he got here."

"That may be so," replied Mycroft. "Heinrich Milch and his issue stand to inherit a large sum if they can prove their descent from Arthur Milligan."

"Well, that makes a change from the sort of request I have had to spend most of my time dealing with these day," grunted Klein. "Most people come here to establish that they are of pure German descent. That's why there are queues waiting to see my colleagues and me. I've never been so busy, and I only took this job because I thought it would give me a quiet life. Our new racial purity laws mean that we all are all having to trace our descent back to 1750. Have you heard the joke about the four most desirable women in Germany?"

Mycroft was not a man given to jest and he looked blank, but Klein was anxious to tell him anyway.

"Four Aryan great-grand-mothers is the answer. A complete set gives you full citizen rights. Having even only one Jewish great-grand-father – which, if my understanding is correct, means you are not actually a Jew according to Jewish law – debars you from all public office and from practising any of the professions. Goodness knows what our new masters will come up with next."

"What the German government does is of no matter to me," said Mycroft carelessly. "This is a simple intestacy case. Milligan is an Irish name – names that end with the letters 'AN' often are – and the Milligans came from county Cork in the south of

Ireland. So do you have any birth or death certificates with the name Milch? I suppose it is possible that they might have reverted to the name Milligan or switched to some other name at some point."

"Milch actually sounds quite Jewish," mused Klein, as he climbed a ladder to get to a top shelf. "Jews were forced to take surnames, and some were given pleasant sounding names like Rosental and Grünwald which mean rose valley and green wood. Some were given insulting names like Klutz or Katzenellbogen which mean fool and cat's elbow. And some were given names that sound normal but a bit odd – Milch, as we have discussed, means milk and there's that physicist with the name Einstein or One stone."

He came down with a file and sat before us.

"Most people," he continued, "are very anxious to find out that they have no Jewish connection, and it was the first thing I checked about myself when this government came to power. Strange world we live in. Germans are meant to be blond, tall, and athletic. Our government talks of nothing else and of the requirement to improve the breeding stock. And look what we have got as leaders. We are led by the mousy-haired Hitler, the runty Goebbels, and the grossly overweight Göring. Der dicke Hermann is the nickname we give him. You really couldn't make it up."

He put an end to his musings.

"I found no Milligans among our Ms up there," he said, "and this one file contains the only reference I have to a family called

Milch. Here is the birth certificate of an Erhard Milch who was born here in 1892. His father was listed as Anton Milch, who is described here as an apothecary born in Krefeld and, as I suspected, a Jew who has converted to Christianity. That will ruin someone's day, though having some Jewish ancestry is actually quite common as there have been Jews in Germany for centuries. Anton Milch's wife and the mother of the child is named as Klara Vetter, which sounds a very German name. So nothing relevant to your Henry Milligan."

"Could you tell me something about these Milchs just in case there is some connection."

I think Klein was slightly surprised by this response, but he continued.

"I said that Anton Milch was a baptised Jew. They lived at what was then Kaiser Strasse 12 which is not far from here. The Friedrichshafen town council have changed the road name to Horst Wessel Strasse after a man called Horst Wessel. Our new masters regard Wessel as a hero but he actually ran prostitutes in Berlin and led the local branch of the Sturmabteilung – who are basically a bunch of thugs with not enough to do, sorry, did I say that? – but it's only to foreigners that I can say what I think. Well, if any Milchs come here looking into their descent, they will be in for a bit of a shock. Having a Jew as a father will mean Erhard Milch can't keep his jobs in the public services if that's where he works even if his father had become a Christian. But I'm afraid I can't help you with your Irish connection at all."

Mycroft thanked Herr Klein with a charm I would not have suspected, but which may have had something to do with him displaying the same thespian skills as his brother so often showed. He retained the dispassionate face of a lawyer for as long as we were in the registry but, once back on the street, his demeanour was cast in shadows.

"I am not sure what I can do now to protect Milch. Information about his descent is easily obtainable and very clear."

We sat on a bench outside the registry, and he took a pinch of snuff.

"Let us go to what is now the Horst Wessel Strasse and see if any Milchs still live there. If they do not, it may be the easiest place to find where they are now," he said.

Horst Wessel Strasse was a wide and well-to-do street with houses with gardens on both sides. To save the postman time, the houses had boxes for mail at their gate. Adopting a tactic that might have been used by his brother, Mycroft fished into the box at number 12 and took out an envelope. "We are fortunate indeed, Doctor," he said as he looked at it. "Even over forty years after the birth of Herr Erhard Milch, representatives of the Milch family still live here."

We went up the garden path.

As we approached the house, we heard the sound of loud arguing.

"Niemals!" I head a female voice cry which I knew meant, "Never!" I heard this repeated word repeated several times.

We knocked and the voices broke off. A tall strong-looking blond man of about forty came to the door.

"Sind Sie Erhard Milch?" asked Mycroft.

"Ja," confirmed our interlocutor, looking taken aback.

The rest of what followed was largely conducted in German, but I will render it entirely in English for ease of comprehension.

"My name is Mycroft Holmes."

Was it defiance, was it fear that came over the face of the man before us?

"Good God! What is the brother of the great Sherlock Holmes doing here? You had better come in. I had no idea that our authorities had sought the services of the British state to help enforce our racial purity laws."

"That is not why I am here, Herr Milch," said Mycroft as Milch led us into a comfortably furnished reception room where an elderly and tearful lady sat in an armchair.

"I assume," said Milch, "that you heard the shouting between my mother and me. I suspect the subject we were arguing about is connected with what you are about to say."

"I am here to say that there are suspicions about your racial background which if proven by the authorities here, will disqualify you from office. I have been able to confirm that the suspicions are true."

"Of course they are true. It is a matter you can find out in a few minutes. I am planning to thwart the investigations so that the matter resolves itself."

"That may be wise, but could I ask you to elaborate?"

"The man named as my father on my birth certificate was a Jew who has converted to Christianity called Anton Milch. I am trying to persuade my mother here to sign an affidavit which states that I am the product of an illicit union."

"Niemals! Niemals!" broke in Frau Milch vehemently.

"Mother, if you will not listen to me, please listen at least to what our visitor, Mr Mycroft Holmes, has to say."

"Herr Mycroft Holmes," interjected Frau Milch, "to have the brother of the great Sherlock Holmes in my house is an unparalleled honour. To you I will listen as I respect your judgement. But I will not accept the judgement of my son who wants to dishonour me and disown his birthright."

"Perhaps, Herr Milch," said Mycroft, "you can explain what you wanted your mother to sign up to."

"He wants me to say that he was the result of an illicit and incestuous union between me and my uncle Karl, who was the brother of my mother," interrupted Frau Milch before her son could speak. "He wants me to say…" here she nodded at her son… "that my husband's family was full of insane relatives, but that my husband wanted children. Me having a relationship with my Uncle Karl was a way of giving my husband children and of ending the Milch bloodline."

I confess this sounded more *outré* than anything I had ever heard about in any of the cases I had previously investigated with my friend Sherlock Holmes and even Mycroft looked taken aback.

"Yes," insisted Milch, "my mother has already been able to prove her racial purity back to 1750 and, obviously, the same applies to her Uncle Karl who is her uncle by blood and not by marriage. Such requests are so common these days, that investigation can be done in short order. Here is a picture of my uncle when he was about the age I am now, and you will see he looks very like me. And attributing my siring to Uncle Karl has the advantage that he died in 1906 and cannot deny the relationship. My mother can also say she was impressed by Karl's wealth so this relationship will not impinge on her honour."

"It is not true! It is not true!" objected Frau Milch vehemently.

"Mother, any other solution is much much worse and with this affidavit I can continue to serve my country at the air-ministry. Anything else makes you look like a harlot and, obviously, we cannot say my father was anyone who is still alive as they will deny it."

"And you have no concerns about working for a government which imposes laws that make you have to have recourse something like this, Herr Milch?" asked Mycroft.

"Germany has been dishonoured, and I am above all a patriot. I will do whatever is needed to serve my country and restore it to its rightful place on the world stage."

So sincere were the words of Milch that they quite disarmed anything more that Mycroft might have had to say.

"I really think you had better sign, Frau Milch," I heard Mycroft say, there was a scratching of pen on paper, and soon Mycroft and I were on our way out of the front-door.

"I do not think this is the end of the matter, Doctor," said Mycroft as walked back down the garden path to the road. "The solution Milch has pressed for and effected is questionable in so many respects. And yet, when one reads his record, it is hard to imagine anyone else better suited to the role of secretary to the air-ministry. His appointment to his post is a rational one. Therefore, the man who appointed him must be rational. Let us go to Berlin to see Hermann Göring."

Friedrichshafen to Berlin is a long journey and it was two days before we were in the German capital. As so often before, the presentation of a visiting card, with the name Holmes on it – whether coupled with Sherlock or Mycroft – this time at the reception of Germany's enormous air-ministry building, was sufficient to get us swift access to the key person in this drama and we were soon in the grandiose office of the German Reichsmarschall, Hermann Göring.

"I am here to see you about your deputy, Erhard Milch," said Mycroft.

"Good God!" exclaimed Göring, who must have tipped the scales at over twenty stone, and whose girth dwarfed what would otherwise have been an enormous desk. "So that was where Felchner was last week. I was told he had gone to London, but I had no idea why. Now I understand what he was looking for there."

I am sure that this was not the response Mycroft had been expecting, and he stayed silent.

"Let me guess," continued Göring. "Felchner has been pushing for promotion since I started here two years ago. He asks me about it all the time. He is loyal, hard-working, and very stupid. I assume he has told you, just as he says to me every day, that the man in the position he wants is of Jewish origin."

Göring broke off and then looked earnestly at us.

"I must tell you gentleman, Felchner has been bleating to me about Erhard Milch every day for months. He will not leave me in peace."

Mycroft remained silent, stunned, as I was, by the turn matters had taken.

"Mr Mycroft Holmes," Göring went on, "it is truly an honour to have you here and this may be news to you, but what we are discussing is something that happens here all the time. It is rather like your brother's attempt to rough up the blackmailer Charles Augustus Milverton. Milverton said he had hoped your brother would try something original. I thought when your card came up that it would relate to a matter slightly out of the ordinary. I spend half my life dealing with this sort of nonsense although I concede Felchner's move to involve you has taken matters in a direction that is novel – much as *The Red Headed League* was a novel method of staging something as trite as a bank robbery."

Göring sat back in his chair.

"I expect your brother – I must admit to a slight sense of disappointment that I am not meeting him as well, Herr Mycroft Holmes and Herr Dr Watson – would at this point light his pipe and have a ponder. But in this ministry we have banned smoking. We are the first public building in Europe to do so. I am a recovering morphine addict, but I understand from the writings of Dr Watson here that he has even weaned your brother off his hallucinogenic drugs entirely. How very tedious that all is! There is nothing to stimulate us at all."

Mycroft remained silent and Göring continued.

"You have stumbled across one of the problems with our great project here in Germany, gentlemen. We have tried to give jobs to everyone, so we have one form of security force after another – the regular army which we call the Wehrmacht, the Schutzstaffel which we call the SS, the Leibstandarte which is Herr Hitler's personal bodyguard, and the Sturmabteilung. The list goes on and on. That is what we have done to reflate our economy. But there are never enough top jobs to go round so people look for other ways to climb what I think you English call the greasy pole."

"Pray continue."

"One of the most popular ways to do so is to claim that the person whose position you aspire to is of Jewish origin and then to denounce them. I must say that Felchner has shown an ingenuity I would not have attributed to him to approach you. I assume that Felchner asked you to check on the background of Milch, his superior, thinking that I would believe you when I had previously refused to act on Felchner's concerns when he had expressed them to me directly."

"Herr Milch," said Mycroft cautiously, "has got his mother to sign an affidavit that he was the result of an incestuous relationship between his mother and her uncle."

"Now that too is original," said Göring, his look of ennui partly clearing. "I have always regarded Milch as the cleverest of my subordinates. Mostly in this situation I hear that the child was the result of a coupling with an unknown partner. It is amazing how often German women have been unfaithful to their Jewish husbands with men who cannot be traced. And the other way round as well. Lots of men with Jewish wives seem to have picked up undocumented children from orphanages." He paused. "Perhaps we could use that as a mean to persuade the Germans to institute divorce proceedings against their Jewish spouses. To involve an uncle, who I assume is conveniently deceased so cannot be questioned…"

"Karl Brauer died in 1906," said Mycroft, sounding slightly forlorn.

"…is a touch I have never previously had before me. I must confess to being not quite sure that I can cross my legs quite often enough when I think about a coupling between a young woman and her aged uncle. I am not sure that Rassenschande…"

"…That is a relationship between a German and a non-German," explained Mycroft to me, "the term means 'racial disgrace…'"

"...Is any worse than that. And," Göring continued, "may I commend you, Herr Mycroft Holmes, on your command of German expressions of very recent provenance."

I cannot think of any case in which I was involved with a denouement anything like this one and Mycroft was silent. In the end I felt it fell to me to speak next.

"What is to happen now?"

"We have a lot of war graves that need attending to in France. Felchner has got sufficiently on my nerves with his ceaseless efforts to get Milch's job that I will make them his principal responsibility and leave Milch free to focus on the important stuff. The German war-graves authority is in Cologne which is on the other side of the country so he will have to relocate there, and I will have him out of my hair at last. Sometimes a man can go too far."

"And what is to happen to Milch?" I pressed.

"I am not sure I understand the question, Dr Watson. Milch is an excellent subordinate and is the stand-out candidate for his role. There are not many people who can offer experience like he has in civil aviation. This air-ministry is anxious to build up this country's air power – it hardly needs saying, for civil purposes only, though we use a wide interpretation of what constitutes civil aviation – and Milch is one of the top brains in the land. So of course I want him here in my ministry. I have important work for him to do."

Göring's desk was clear apart from an imposing wooden cabinet on it. It was to this cabinet to which Göring now turned.

He opened it and pulled out an elaborate looking piece of paper studded with stamps and markings which he proceeded to sign.

"To put an end to all inquiries on this topic, I will issue Milch with a certificate confirming his German origin. We give these certificates a catchy name – Deutschblütigkeitserklärungen. There's another expression you can add to your German vocabulary, Mr Holmes. It means a declaration of German blood. It is rather ironic we call it that as we give it to those whose German blood is questionable. Issuing these is something I have the power to do, and it will stop any further inquiries being initiated. Milch also has a job to do, and he can now do without having to worry that some subordinate like Felchner – loyal to the German state but thick as.. well, Dr Watson, as thick as any comparator you would like to insert at this point – will seek to undermine him. Milch is not the first person I have issued such a certificate to, and I am sure he will not be the last."

The sound of another pen scratching on paper and then Göring looked up at us.

"It is I, gentlemen, who decides who are the Jews around here."

Soon Mycroft and I were on our way back in London. The British Government's most senior advisor looked quite put out by what had happened. "If the Germans are capable of taking decisions which put pragmatism over dogma, then that will greatly complicate our dealings with them over the next years to come."

A few years later my second wife died, I sold my practice, and I took once more to sharing quarters with Sherlock Holmes. With Mycroft's permission, I briefed my friend on matters that Mycroft and I had worked on and, as my readers may imagine, the investigation of Erhard Milch and the ensuing meeting with Göring caused us to follow events in Germany and in particular the careers of Hermann Göring and of Erhard Milch with keen interest.

Göring remained at the top of the National Socialist tree until Germany surrendered in 1945 while Milch rose to be a field-marshal. At the end of the war Milch was taken prisoner by British troops who had just seen the horror of the Belsen Concentration Camp. They gave him a thorough beating and broke his skull. He was subsequently given a life-sentence for his use of slave-labour in aircraft manufacture.

When the war ended, Sherlock Holmes and I were asked to go to Germany – he to assist with the interrogation of the most senior surviving National Socialist leaders and I to play my customary role as his amanuensis.

By the time we saw Göring in October 1946, the former Reichsmarschall had already been condemned to hang, and, having lost a quarter of his weight compared to when I had last seen him, he was far from the ebullient figure whom Mycroft and I had met in 1935. Sherlock Holmes and I were alone with him in his cell accompanied only by a prison-guard called Greenwood.

"I shall probably dangle at the end of the rope for twenty minutes or so before I finally expire," said Göring to us. "I fear it is all going to be rather unpleasant. Surely you, Mr Holmes, can still intervene for me and point out that I did my best to mitigate some of the less attractive aspects of the National Socialist regime, and that I do not deserve to hang. Erhard Milch was not the only person I protected."

"I think it was you who came up with the idea of the Jews in Germany paying a billion Reichsmarks as a communal fine after the Night of Broken Glass," countered Holmes.

"That was a measure levied on the whole population," replied Göring, "and there were colleagues – Ribbentrop in the cell next door and Goebbels, now dead – who wanted to levy a higher sum. I was able to help in individual cases, and I did so when I could, as was the case with Milch."

The death sentence had already been passed, and Holmes was not there to help Göring with his problems, but when later that same month the American prison-guards came to take Göring to the gallows, they found he had already taken poison. Several different people have been identified as the possible providers of that poison – indeed Holmes and I were subject to questioning about it. For my own part, I cannot help wondering if the prison guard Greenwood who was the only witness to the discussions between Göring, Holmes, and me took the view that Göring had sufficient redeeming features that he should escape the fate of being hanged and procured the poison for him.

Eva and the Woman from Swastika

And yet my brother has said of me that my specialism is omniscience.

In this most public and mysterious affair I set down now – far too grave to entrust to any amanuensis – I am far from certain that this is an accurate description of me as the tide of events took me far from my normal areas of expertise.

It was on the evening of the 21st of August 1939 that the bellhop of the Diogenes club came to me at my normal station in the club library with a note which said, "There is a young lady waiting for you at reception." As we walked to the reception he murmured, "I think she's German, Mr Holmes. I couldn't make out a name and she speaks no English. She's waiting for you in the Stranger's Room."

My visitor was about five foot four, slim, blond, and in her late twenties. I suspect a mind focused on matters lowlier than statecraft might have applied the word "pretty" to her. My readers will note I do not use the word "client" to refer to her as someone who seeks me out for help is likely to have a matter of far greater moment than the trivial matters of the police court my brother's clients brought before him.

Young Sherlock was capable of quoting Goethe in the original to Dr Watson. I would categorise my brother's German as no better than mine so the lack of English of the person I was about to see posed no problem and the discussions that followed were conducted in her native tongue.

Under her arm was a bulky volume which, rather to my disappointment, I saw to be the complete works of Dr Watson about my brother.

The fear rose in my mind that I was going to be asked for an autograph but in the event she introduced herself as Fräulein Eva Braun and started to speak.

"I went to Baker Street," she began, "and there I said the name "Herr Holmes" to Frau Hudson. Your brother's landlady got this book down from the shelf and a map of England. She pointed to the name Sherlock Holmes and pointed at the map to somewhere far to the south of London. She then pointed to your name and to this address from *Der griechische Dolmetscher*" – it took me a second to remember that a Dolmetscher is the German word for an interpreter and that it was *The Greek Interpreter* that my visitor was talking about. "I take it that you are Herr Mycroft Holmes. The taxi driver found the Diogenes easily when I asked him and here I am."

I nodded and the thought passed through my head that if Mrs Hudson was able to show someone with whom she shared no common language where I might be found, this might not be the last visitor I got.

I looked at her again. What could this woman be seeking from a man already in his tenth decade?

"I am the girl-friend of the Führer," she said.

By 1939 it was, of course, impossible not to know to whom Fräulein Braun was referring with the word the Führer although that the German leader had an amatory companion was news to me. I have been a life-long bachelor and have speculated that having such an amatory companion might obtrude on my judgement of human affairs which is why I have never indulged in such a thing myself.

I put aside these thoughts to concentrate on Fräulein Braun.

"I understand, Mr Holmes, that you are even cleverer than your brother Sherlock," said she, a slightly coquettish smile on her face.

I am not sure whether this remark was meant to win my sympathy but confined myself to opining, "One must treat everything that appears in the somewhat meretricious works of Dr Watson with a degree of scepticism."

"I am at my wit's end, Herr Holmes, and that is why I am come to London. The Führer has taken up with another woman."

There are many across whose face a slightly salacious smile might have spread as they learned of this thus unknown side of the German leader, but I flatter myself that I remained expressionless.

"I am not allowed to be photographed with him," she continued, a note of complaint coming into her voice. "When I am in government buildings I am not permitted into the public areas. No one knows who I am or what my status is. The Führer makes no public display of affection towards me. He will not even acknowledge my existence."

She paused and was overcome by what I suppose was a surge of emotion. I asked one of the attendants to bring her a glass of water and she continued.

"I am a void. If I were the wife of your king or of the American president, I would be well-known, and on the cover of every magazine. And now, with me having done everything that he has asked of me, now he consorts with someone else. She is known among the Führer's circle as the Valkyrie. And she looks the part, including her legs. Here I am, the mistress of the greatest man in Germany and in the whole world, and I am forced to sit there waiting while the sun mocks me through the windowpanes."

How the discussions had developed so far was completely outside the ambit of my experience and I was about to say so when Fräulein Braun continued.

"My rival is an English woman, Herr Holmes. I was hoping that a man as clever as you or your brother" – I decided to let this comparison between my somewhat intellectually challenged brother and me pass – "might be able to help me, a simple German girl, find a way. And," she added, with what many would regard as a winning smile, "you are an Englishman so you may have a greater understanding of a woman such as her than I do."

"I fear Madame," I said at last, "that what you are asking me is quite beyond where I might be able to help you. I have not the least experience I can bring to bear on the matter you have related. My focus, intellectual and otherwise, is entirely on statecraft."

Discussions continued for a while as Fräulein Braun tried to persuade me to become involved in this affair of the heart.

In the end it was only by agreeing to take this photograph and an address in Bavaria where I might write to her if I had a change of mind that I was able to persuade her to leave at all.

Fräulein Braun had barely gone when the bellhop approached me again with another note announcing the presence of a visitor. I feared Miss Braun might have returned or that her rival in the Führer's affections might have arrived, but instead, waiting for me at reception was the Foreign Secretary Lord Halifax and alongside him one of the officials of the club – I think the chairman of the committee for preventing social interaction."

It was the club official who spoke first.

"I trust that having two visitors in one evening to our club which is designed for the most unclubbable men in London, will not become a regularity, Mr Holmes," said he in a forbidding and authoritative voice. "This club is a tolerant place, but it does have its rules. The apostrophe in the designation, 'Stranger's Room', comes before rather than after the 's' for a reason."

He left and I found myself alone with the tall and austere Lord Halifax. In my long involvement in the government of this country I had of course dealt with Halifax before. He had earned the sobriquet "The Holy Fox" because of his piety and shrewdness although I had always taken the view that whatever his Lordship's godliness, his reputation for shrewdness was founded on my own management of the body politic, and this was why he had been forced to consult with me now.

"I am somewhat at a loss where to turn to," started Halifax, blustering slightly. "It is a matter of statecraft…"

"Of that I am the master…" I interrupted.

"..and of the heart," he added.

There was a pause, and I forbore to make any remark although I could feel my own robust but distinctly wooden heart sinking. I seemed to be being faced with the wholly unwelcome prospect of becoming a counsellor to the love-sick.

"The woman in this matter is a cousin once removed of the wife of Mr Winston Churchill," went on Halifax. I confess my spirits soared at the prospect of being consulted on a milieu of which I had some understanding.

"The former Chancellor of the Exchequer and the present Member of Parliament for Epping?" I asked taken aback. "He is often spoken of as a future Prime Minister."

"The same. The woman in question is called Miss Unity Mitford. She has spent most of the last five years in Munich. Intelligence reports tell us that much of that time is spent with the German leader, Herr Hitler."

There was a pause and my spirits which had soared sank once more for I could see where this was leading.

"All of our intelligence, ever since Hitler came to power, has indicated that he has no interest in matters of the heart at all. And now we have an English woman who seems to be able to penetrate Hitler's inner circle at will."

I was far from sure whether Halifax had got his last sentence quite the right way around but let the matter pass.

My reader will understand that I now debated internally whether I should tell Lord Halifax about my previous visitor but decided to preserve the confidentiality of what I suppose my brother would have called a consultation and I confess that I have no better term.

"What can you tell me about her, My Lord?" I asked instead.

"She was born in 1914, so she is in her mid-twenties. Here is a picture of her." Halifax handed me the picture on the left showing a young woman with a notably determined jut to her jaw.

"She is of a family which can trace its descent to Norman times," the Foreign Secretary continued. "She has a brother and five sisters. One of her sisters, Diana, has taken up with Oswald Mosley, who is leader of the British Union of Fascists, while another is an ardent and active Communist. The whole family is a collection of extremists."

Halifax seemed to be in the grip of a massive of internal conflict and the next remark came *sotto voce*. "Really, the idea of a noble family of this country cosying up to the leader of the

German National Socialist Party which is intent on gobbling up every country in Europe – well, it doesn't really bear thinking about."

"What is it you want me to do, My Lord?"

"I need you to go to Munich, to find out what is going on between Miss Mitford and the German leader. I need you then to provide an opinion on what, if anything, can be done to turn the matter to this country's advantage. If she could prevail on her lover to stop invading other countries, that would be of great value. If she could be persuaded to spy for us, that might be of greater value still. You may keep that photograph and use it as a means of identifying her."

If my caller had wanted to present a petition designed to appeal to my brother, he would have referred to vague, abstract, and doubtless very worthy concepts like "love of truth" or "desire for justice". Given what I knew of the capabilities of Lord Halifax, I thought it highly unlikely he would have had the emotional intelligence to couch his appeal to me in a way that I would find hard to resist, but, irrespective of how he had come upon the formulation he had chosen, being presented with the opportunity to "turn the matter to this country's advantage" made the matter completely irresistible to me.

The decision in Germany to grant the vote to women, as in so many countries, after the Great War, I mused, had had many consequences. I had always fancied that Herr Hitler cultivated his image as an unattached man as a means of attracting the female vote which was well over 50% of the electorate in Germany because of the loss of men in the Great War of twenty-five years previously. Would, I speculated, the revelation in the press outside Germany that Hitler was as prone to a loss of amatory self-control as most of the rest of mankind, reduce his hold over the German people? Such information would leak back into Germany soon enough whatever controls the German authorities might have over the locally published press.

I interrupted these thoughts to return to matters of practicality.

"But I cannot go to Munich to track down this Mitford woman without knowing where I might find her."

"The headquarters of the National Socialist Party are in a building called the *Das braune Haus* or the Brown House. It is number 45 on a road which used to be called the Brennerstraße but which, like so many of the major throughfares in German cities, is now called the Adolf Hitler Straße. Although it is rendered in white stucco, the house is called the Brown House because of the National Socialist Party's colour. It is striking how often the colour brown features in discussions of the party. Braunau-am-Inn, which is where Herr Hitler was born, means brown pasture by the river Inn, which is a tributary of the Danube."

As Lord Halifax made his observation about the colour brown and the striking frequency of its appearance in matters relating to the National Socialist Party and Herr Hitler, I wondered whether he would also reference Fräulein Braun, whose name, as my readers will know, means Miss Brown. His failure to do so, confirmed to me – not at all to my surprise – that he knew nothing about Miss Mitford's rival in the German leader's affections, or, I surmised perhaps a little cruelly, about much else.

"Hitler is often in Munich," Halifax continued, "although his movements are not made public so I cannot guarantee he will be there when you arrive, and you will have to bide your time. London will be waiting for your word."

"How can I provide you with my thoughts when I am in Munich."

"Munich is a large enough city to have a British Consulate. You should send any messages from there so that they can be encoded."

This was as vague a commission as any of the footling matters my brother had ever received but, in no longer than it took to pack a bag, I was on my way to Victoria Station, and the evening of the next day saw me checking into Munich's Hotel Regina. I went for a constitutional walk after my long journey. The late summer weather was beautiful but what struck me most on the street was how so many of the men and boys I saw were in brown uniforms – it was as if the Boy Scouts movement had taken over the country and the boys' fathers had joined up as well. I half expected to hear choruses of, "Dib, dib, dib! Dub, dub, dub!".

I sought out the National Socialist Party's headquarters on the following morning. The building was an imposing one on three stories with the flag of the National Socialist Party – a swastika on a white square with a red surround, although in truth such flags were everywhere to be seen in Munich – fluttering on the top. That and the brown-uniformed guards – no surprise to find even more men in dun colours, I mused – standing at the gate and at the door were the only indication of what it was. There was a café opposite, so I took my station there and watched. "It could," I said to myself, "all be a waste of time. Berlin is the German capital city, and Hitler may not even be here in Munich."

But, remarkably, I was wrong.

At twelve o'clock the guards at the front of the building stood to one side and, as I watched, Hitler appeared at the top of the steps. He was in company – Göring from his burly frame, I could recognise, though not the others. When the party was complete, Hitler and his colleagues came down the steps of the building, through the gate, and started to walk down the road.

I hurriedly paid for my coffee and followed them at a distance.

I did not have far to go, for Hitler and his party soon turned into a restaurant on the junction of Schellingstraße and Schraudolphstraße called Osteria Bavaria. I strolled past and glanced inside as discreetly as I could. There was the German leader at a table at the back of the restaurant with his party. There seemed to be no particular security precautions – indeed, as I looked, I noticed other lunchtime diners who apparently had nothing to do with the National Socialists. I thought about going in myself, but I felt I would be better off observing and so repaired to another café to watch.

After an hour, the party came out, and all except one member of the group headed back towards the party headquarters.

The exception was a young woman who walked briskly in the opposite direction and whom I recognised as Miss Mitford. She must have been inside the restaurant wating for Hitler's party when it arrived, I concluded. She disappeared around a corner and had gone from sight by the time I got there.

So this was where Hitler and his leadership team went for lunch. And Miss Mitford must live close by as the street she had turned into was a residential one.

So how was I, a man in his nineties, going to scrape an acquaintance with a twenty-four- year-old woman?

I spent the afternoon reflecting on this problem and in the end I decided that the best thing to do was to go for lunch to the Osteria Bavaria the next day.

As my brother commented in *The Blanched Soldier* – a rare instance in the Canon of a matter which he narrates entirely himself – the advantage of having a chronicler like Dr Watson is that you can keep him in a constant state of surprise, and he can convey that surprise to the readers to keep them agog as to what might be happening next. As I here am acting as my own chronicler, my readers will have to forgive me if, to create what I understand to be known in the writing trade as "suspense", I keep the plan I had formulated to myself.

I confess that it goes against the grain for me to try to build this so-called "suspense" in what I regard as an academic textbook on statecraft but, if this account if events is ever read, there will, I suppose, be some need to pander to the predilections of less intellectual readers.

I got to the Osteria at half-past-eleven, took a seat opposite the door, and then sat contemplating the menu.

As someone who is used to dining on their own, I took matters at a leisurely pace. "I am here to enjoy myself and savour the atmosphere," I said to the waiter in English as he asked me whether he could bring me anything.

"We are the oldest restaurant in Munich," he replied, "Feel free to take your time. You are not the only one who comes here as much for the experience as for the meal."

At a quarter to twelve a woman whom I recognised as Unity Mitford arrived and took her place at another table.

She too seemed to want to take her time before ordering and she too seemed to be staring at the door.

At about ten-past-twelve she called the waiter over and said in strikingly good German, "Kommt der Führer heute nicht?" or "Is the Führer not coming today." For ease of reading, I recount the rest of the dialogue in English.

The waiter responded, "He sent a message to say that he is gone back to Berlin, Miss Mitford and so will not be coming today."

"But he reserved a table here yesterday," countered Miss Mitford, looking distressed.

The waiter shrugged.

"At least he cancelled his reservation which many would not do. It is very kind of him to be so considerate when he has so many demands on his time. And it is very like him too."

At this point I collapsed forward onto my table clutching my heart.

Miss Mitford and the waiter rushed over.

"Are you alright, sir?" asked the waiter in English. "Can I get you some water?"

I sat up hesitantly.

"Is he English?" I heard Miss Mitford ask of the waiter in German.

"He spoke English to me when he asked for a menu, but he could be from anywhere outside the Reich as I could not tell if it were a non-Englishman speaking English."

"Have you seen him before?"

"No, this is his first time here as far as I know."

It was time for me to speak.

"A temporary moment of weakness," I whispered hoarsely. "It happens when you get to my age. If I could have a glass of water, I am sure I will be fine."

The waiter brought over some water, and I sipped it hesitantly.

"I am in Munich as a tourist," I said faintly. "My wife died last year, and I am taking advantage of these my last years to tour Europe."

"Perhaps you might sit with our sick Englishman and keep an eye on him, Fräulein Mitford," suggested the waiter.

"Thank you," I said, panting slightly. "That would be a huge comfort to me although, as I said, I am sure I will be fine. I get these attacks from time to time, and it is a small matter. Indeed," I said, sitting properly upright, and reverting to something like my normal voice, "I feel my appetite return and I will have another look at the menu. Fräulein Mitford," I added, "if you will stay with me and accompany me back to my hotel afterwards, I will happily invite you to lunch. At my age and in my condition, you need fear no impropriety."

No time at all seemed to pass before Fräulein Mitford, or Miss Mitford as she asked me to call her, and I were sat over a fine meal.

"So what are you doing in Munich?" I asked.

"I am studying German."

"And you are doing very well," I said, dredging up from somewhere a charm I have rarely needed to deploy. "I speak a little German myself and what you said to the waiter sounded fluent."

Miss Mitford blushed slightly but looked pleased and said, "It was but a small matter as I have now lived here for several years."

"And how long do you plan to stay?"

"Well, I came with the intention of only being here for a few months, but I find myself staying longer and longer. I have been fortunate in the people I have met."

"And you eat at the same restaurant as the German leader."

"He and I are –" she paused as she sought the right word, "– acquainted. Herr Hitler has always been most kind to me. We speak when he comes here and elsewhere, although I have to be careful about my association with him. I can tell you this as an Englishman, but Herr Hitler and I can never be seen in company together. I could not even say that much to a German. But when I told him I wanted to stay in Munich, he found me a flat so that we could…" she paused to consider what to say next. A slight reddish hue passed over her features as she continued, "so that I would have a place I could call my own and receive visitors."

"That is a remarkable gesture for the leader of a nation towards a foreign national."

"Well, it belonged to some Jews, but they were being expropriated, so it was easy for him to arrange," she said with a shrug of indifference. "But it was still kind of him to take the time. As I was preparing to move in, I could hear the owner's wife crying in the room next door as I organized the redecoration of the living-room that had belonged to her. I can't say I felt sorry for her though. She had had the flat for a long time."

I was not sure how to respond to this and decided to change the focus of our conversation.

"What do you think of Herr Hitler's politics?"

A distant look came into Miss Mitford's eyes.

"I first became aware of them six years ago when I went with my sister Diana, her husband, Oswald, and other members of the British Union of Fascists to the Nuremburg rally. There were two-hundred-thousand people there cheering for Hitler. Truly he is the greatest man there has ever been. He has saved Germany from its enemies and Europe from Communism which is an alien philosophy thought up by a Jew for the benefit of the Jews."

Again, I had no idea how to respond to this and changed the subject once more.

"And how long do you plan to stay in Munich?"

"I have no plans to return to Great Britain for the moment. I see myself as a bridge between our two great nations. I was conceived in a town called 'Swastika' in Canada where my parents were following a business opportunity. And look at all the flags with swastikas around us. My first name is Unity, and I unite two countries. My second name is Valkyrie because my grand-father was a friend of Richard Wagner, who is the Führer's favourite composer. And I am a Mitford who can trace her lineage back a thousand years to the Normans. It is hard not to see all this as fate. In the end, I suppose, I would like to see a parade on Whitehall in London or on Unter den Linden in Berlin led by both the King and by Herr Hitler. I would feel my life's work would then be done."

"And you feel no anti-British hostilities here?"

"Oh no indeed. The Führer has often expressed his admiration for the British and how a country of Britain's size has built an empire greater than any the world has yet seen."

I could not see how Miss Mitford's close association with Hitler might be turned to Britain's advantage as if any conflict between her loyalties arose I was sure she would back the German side.

I nevertheless found Miss Mitford a curiosity and discussions continued until we had finished our meal.

She walked me back to my hotel and I was amused to see she failed to notice Herr Hitler and his entourage eating at the charming-looking Füchschen or Little Fox, round the corner from the Osteria Bavaria, as we walked past. This was where I had suggested to the Party they go when I rang the Brown House pretending I was from the Osteria Bavaria which had suffered a plumbing leak and recommending a different place for them to try. As my reader might expect, the next call that the Brown House got was from Füchschen placing its hospitality at the Führer's disposal. As well as both these calls, the one which had told the Osteria Bavaria that Hitler had been forced to go back to Berlin had of course also come from me.

After I had got back to my hotel and Miss Mitford had left me, I went to the British Consulate, and telegraphed Lord Halifax in Munich to tell him that there was no point in trying to get Miss Mitford interested in being a spy for Great Britain. His response was swift. "Talks in Moscow for miliary alliance with Soviets near conclusion. That will stop the Germans! Need for new spy in Germany much reduced".

I decided to return home but the train to London was not until the following morning.

It was as I was checking out of the hotel the next day that a messenger dashed up to me and said, "You're needed at the Consulate, sir. Please come at once."

When I got there it was to find the building abuzz.

"There's a phone call been arranged for you with Lord Halifax, Mr Holmes," said the consul. "It's on a special scrambled line."

When Halifax came on it was to say, "The Germans have got in ahead of us. They have done a deal with the Soviets. They describe it as a non-aggression pact. Why did no one tell us that this was going on? Get hold of Miss Mitford and see if she is more likely to spy for us now that Hitler has done a deal with the Communists."

I must admit I rather doubted the wisdom of this. Miss Mitford seemed so smitten by Hitler that I was sure she would back an alliance between Hitler and the Devil and that a pact between Hitler and Stalin would not cause her to raise an eyebrow. But as someone who had been a civil servant, I felt I must do whatever my political masters wanted. I could hear Lord Halifax down the telephone say in a world-weary tone, "Things would be so much easier if only Herr Hitler and Stalin had studied at Oxford."

But where was Miss Mitford?

I went back to the Osteria Bavaria armed with a large bunch of flowers – the first time in my long life that I had ever bought a gift for anyone. I said they were for Miss Mitford and that I would like to drop them off at her residence, but the waiter had no idea where she lived although he did say I could leave them with him. I told him I might be back and walked down the street Miss Mitford had turned down when I had seen her emerge from the Osteria. I looked at the name against each bell, but could not find hers. I watched the Osteria Bavaria but neither Miss Mitford nor Hitler went. I was later to discover the Party big-wigs really had now gone to Berlin and I did wonder when I found this out whether it was in the German capital that Miss Mitford might be found.

And then on the morning of Sunday the third of September I found her.

Germany had invaded Poland two days previously and a British and French declaration of war was expected at any time. I had no access to a wireless, so I was not even sure whether a declaration had not in fact already been made. I had taken to patrolling the streets around the Osteria to see if I could spot Miss Mitford. And suddenly there she was! She was pressing the bell at an imposing house and even from over fifty yards away I could see she looked panic-stricken.

As I watched, she was admitted and disappeared inside.

I walked up to the building and saw the name on the bell was that of a Dr Gerber who described himself as a Frauenarzt or gynaecologist.

I was in no doubt as to why Miss Mitford would want to visit such a practitioner and decided that my best interests would be served by following her. I waited in a nearby doorway. Eventually she came out and away she went, walking very slowly, and I in turn came out from concealment and followed her. To my astonishment a figure that I recognised as Fräulein Braun came out from a doorway between Miss Mitford and me and it was obvious she was doing the same.

Munich is not a large city and soon we came to a great park called the Englischer Garten or the English garden stretching north from the centre. My readers may like to speculate on whether this choice of destination was significant, but they may find what happened next more worthy of their consideration.

Miss Mitford came to a halt in a clearing surrounded by trees and stood there motionless.

A shot rang out and she fell to the ground, clearly gravely wounded but not yet dead as I could see her writhing on the ground.

Fräulein Braun ran up to her, stood briefly over Miss Mitford's prostrate form, shouted something I could not understand, and then ran on.

Before I could get to Miss Mitford, two brown-uniformed men emerged from the surrounding trees, and crouched over her.

By the time I had got to her she was lying in a spreading pool of her own blood. One of the men was holding a small pistol by the muzzle. On its pearl handle I could see the intertwined letters AH and UVM and I can only speculate that it was a gift from

Adolf Hitler to Unity Valkyrie Mitford. The gun was not smoking. The brown-shirted men were themselves armed and waved me away as I stood there.

I was not sure what to do, but I had no desire to argue with armed men, and as I got back to the entrance of the park I could hear the wail of a siren which I took to be an approaching ambulance.

I made my way to the British Consulate and the British Consul said, "War was declared this morning, and we must wait on the Germans to see how we can get home. I expect that they will play by the rules and that we will be swapped with their diplomatic staff in London and elsewhere, but I cannot guarantee it, and it will certainly take some time. You should go to your hotel and await further instructions. We have, I fear, no means of communicating with London."

As it was, it was the middle of October before I got back to London. During that time my access to news had been very limited although I found the ambience, cut off from the outside world, rather like the soothing atmosphere of the Diogenes. As soon as I arrived in the British capital, it was to the Diogenes I went to enjoy it further.

I had no sooner resumed my familiar station when Lord Halifax arrived.

"I would that the outbreak of war had obviated the need to do any more about Miss Mitford, but I fear that this is not the case," he said as we sat in Stranger's.

I debated how much I should tell Lord Halifax of what I had seen but in the end confined myself to the familiar refrain of my brother.

"Pray continue."

"She took a bullet in the head on the day war broke out. It did not kill her, and she has been taken to a hospital in Bern in Switzerland and will stay there until she is fit to return to this country."

"What condition is she in?"

"We understand she is mentally incapacitated, but we do not know to what extent or how much of it is reversible."

"Can you explain more about the circumstances of her shooting?" I asked, curious as to how much Lord Halifax knew.

"It is, as you may imagine, rather difficult to get reliable information out from Germany and none of that is now relevant as we and the Germans are now at war. Maybe more details will come out once she is here, but they may not as they will have to come from her, and it will depend on what her recollection of events is."

"And how does she have the means to pay for treatment at the hospital in Switzerland?"

"We understand that Herr Hitler, or plain Hitler as I suppose we should now call him, is paying her hospital bills from his own pocket. When she is ready to be moved, Miss Mitford's mother and one of her sisters will travel out to Switzerland and bring her back to this country."

"And why are you telling me this?"

"We would like you, a man of impeccable reputation and experience and yet not an attention seeker, to accompany the Mitfords to Switzerland and back to ensure fair play. And there is another complicating factor."

"What is that?"

"Miss Mitford is pregnant. From your previous comments and from the payment arrangements I have alluded to, it is likely that Hitler has a child on the way by a minor member of the English aristocracy. The child will be related by marriage to Mr Churchill, who is now First Sea Lord and is one of the obvious candidates to be the next Prime Minister should Mr Chamberlain for any reason need to step down. I confess I have no idea what, if anything, we should do about this."

There was a pause.

"It would be most helpful, Mr Holmes, if you could formulate a plan to get us out of this diplomatic imbroglio."

That Lord Halifax should have no idea about what do on anything hardly came as a surprise to me, but this was so far outside my own area of expertise that I had to give the matter considerable thought.

And now we come to the last act of this drama, and I fear that at this point – though I must own too to some feeling of relief – that my ability to narrate this matter as a work of suspense is outmatched. My readers therefore will therefore get this closing chapter as a dry recollection of events which is in any case how matters should normally be presented.

My first task was to speak with Unity Mitford's sister, Diana, who, as readers will recall, was married to the leader of the British Fascists, Oswald Mosley.

"Mrs Mosley," I said to the former Diana Mitford, "your activities before the outbreak of the emergency have endangered the country. The government would be justified in interning you and your husband for the war's duration. It is still possible that charges of high treason may arise from your conduct and that of your husband."

Mrs Mosley stared wide-eyed at me, and I continued.

"I represent the British government, and I will make you an offer under which you can avoid this fate."

She nodded her assent.

"Your sister is pregnant with the child of Adolf Hitler and is mentally incapacitated. If you accept the child and raise it as your own, you can avoid internment. You must however henceforth lead a life in which you and your husband make no public comment about this offer, the child you will rear, or any other political matter. If you fail to abide by this, you and he will be interned with no further ado for an unspecified period, charges of treason which carry the death penalty will be brought against you both, and you will be subject of a secret trial."

Once Lady Mosley had agreed to this, I mandated that Unity Mitford's return should not happen until the weather had turned cold. When, in early January the snow lay upon the ground, I travelled with Miss Mitford's sister, Deborah, and her mother Sydney, to Berne in Switzerland.

I shall henceforth refer to all members of the Mitford family by their first names to avoid confusion between them.

Sydney and Deborah knew about Unity's pregnancy but none of us knew what Unity's mental state would be.

On the train from Paris to Geneva I was as clear to Sydney and Deborah as I had been to Diana.

"You must do exactly as I tell you. Whether Unity can walk or not, when she is in public she must be on a stretcher and covered with a blanket so that no bulge to her stomach should be seen. As I am a diplomat, I must leave all inter-action with Unity to you. I do not expect to see the young lady at all. My role is to make all necessary arrangements for her repatriation with local officials."

Soon after this Unity Mitford arrived back in this country. As I had mandated, she was lying on a stretcher having travelled from Switzerland on an ambulance train. She was widely photographed in the press, but her midriff was, as instructed, always swathed in a loosely fitting blanket, and there were no comments in the press about anything other than her mental state.

In April 1940 I read that Lady Diana Mosley had been delivered of a son whom she called Max. I will be no more by the time this son comes to adulthood, but I must confess to some feeling of curiosity as to what will become of him.

Historical Note by Henry Durham, historical advisor to *The Redacted Sherlock Holmes*

Unity Mitford died of an infection arising from her head wound in 1948 while details of the fates of Adolf Hitler and Eva Braun will be known to readers.

Max Mosley was born on 13 April 1940. His date of birth is thus entirely consistent with the extraordinary revelations disclosed by Mycroft Holmes in this account of events of the late summer of 1939. Mosley was a businessman, lawyer and, in his younger days, a racing driver who eventually went into the administration of the sport, and became president of the *Fédération Internationale de l'Automobile*.

In 2008, Mosley brought a case against News Group Newspapers which had published in *The News of the World* an account of an orgy he had taken part in with five prostitutes. The newspaper alleged that the orgy was Nazi themed as the prostitutes had worn the uniforms of prison guards. The court found that the newspaper had breached Mosely's privacy, and that the orgy had had no Nazi overtones as the prison guard uniforms had not had Nazi insignia on them. Mosley was awarded £60,000 or USD 80,000 at the 2025 rate.

In May 2021 Mosley was told that he had inoperable and fatal cancer.

He killed himself with a shot to the head the next day.

It is inevitable that the reader will be struck by the coincidence of Adolf Hitler, Unity Mitford, and Max Mosley each dying from a gunshot wound to the head.

Liberation Day

Preface by Mycroft Holmes

Readers of my memoirs may wonder why I chose to encumber myself so often in the matters on which I provide service to the British Government with an amanuensis in the form of Dr Watson.

The good doctor's presence does of course spare me the need to write down an account of the matters he describes and so leaves me free to focus on the practice of statecraft which is my *raison-d'être*. The events described below however also contain an unusual additional feature in that it was the doctor's own activities which enabled me to find a solution to a problem which would have been ruinous to our country's best interests. My brother used quasi biblical terms when he said of the good doctor in *The Hound of the Baskervilles*, that he is not himself luminous, but that he is the conductor of light as, through observing his errors, one may be guided to the truth.

So was the case here.

As readers, whenever it might be, go through the below they will understand the unprecedented nature of the matters which arose. I cannot imagine them ever being repeated. Readers will also understand why the publication of this account of events has been embargoed *sine die*.

An account by Dr John Watson

For my readers the global trade wars of the 1890s will still be a fresh memory.

Business magnate Ronald Crump had been elected President of this country's closest ally, the United States, on a promise to make his nation great again. His deputy, Vice President KT Rance, stood four-square behind him. Scandal had surrounded the President both before and during his election campaign. He had been accused of many private indiscretions, he had been arraigned for felonies, and he had repeatedly declined to publish his tax returns as was the normal practice for candidates to the highest office in the United States. His Vice President had had a troubled childhood but had made his name by publishing a book called *Hic Eulogy*, which had contained some quite outré revelations about his past.

My friend, Mr Sherlock Holmes – alas, now deceased as this case post-dates his violent end in Switzerland – had expressed the wish at the time of the case of *The Noble Bachelor*, that the United States and Great Britain become, "a world-wide country under a flag which shall be a quartering of the Union Jack with the Stars and Stripes". I regarded Holmes's understanding of politics as nugatory, and always treated his statements on it with considerable caution. The election of Mr Crump did nothing to diminish this caution.

I had found paying attention to my patients (or indeed to much else) difficult in the wake of Holmes's death and I had been grateful that one of my neighbours had been accommodating in ministering to them. In my distraction I spent most of my time indoors taking comfort in my pipe and speculating in desultory fashion on the stock market. I had ended up with significant holdings in shares that had generally lost value since I had purchased them. At this time, I confess, the only occasions I used to venture outside was to go to the stockbrokers to make another speculation.

Soon after coming to power, it became clear that President Crump, far from sharing the desire of my friend Sherlock Holmes for close relations between our countries, was more interested in a forging an alliance with Russia. He described the Russian leader, Queen Victoria's son-in-law, Tsar Alexander III, in the most glowing terms, and chastised the leaders of Russia's neighbouring countries which had been menaced by Russia's imperial ambitions.

By contrast, leaders of other countries such as France, Germany, and Austro-Hungary ventured across the Atlantic for talks with the new President in some trepidation for, when they got there, it was to be confronted with demands for customs duties on their exports to the United States. "Tariffs" became the new word in modish circles. Shares on their local *bourses* and on the London and New York stock exchanges tumbled in the aftermath of these demands, sometimes to rise again almost as far as they had fallen, when President Crump, seemingly on a whim, announced he would postpone his impositions or even cancel them altogether. I, along with the rest of my countrymen, wondered what would happen when it was the turn of a representative of the British government to cross the Atlantic.

It was on the evening of 12th of April 1893 that there was a knock on the door of my house in Kensington out of which I ran, in my own somewhat sporadic way, my practice.

As it was beyond the hours of the servants, I went to answer the door myself and found Mycroft Holmes standing on the step. I knew from experience that any resistance on my part to his entering was pointless and he made his way to the drawing room where he sat down in my favourite seat as if by right.

"It is like this," said Mycroft without preamble. "Unlike other countries, we have yet to be summoned across the Atlantic as suppliants to treat with the new American President. Accordingly, we have not been subjected to the humiliating process of having to plead against the imposition of tariffs. This is because I have been engaged in negotiating a trade deal with the new administration in the United States from London. We are one of the world's great trading nations as are they. It thus seems preposterous that our trading should be hobbled by tariffs both here and on their side which serve to make imported goods even more expensive than the home-produced equivalents."

I was not sure where this was leading.

It felt inappropriate to ask for more information by echoing my late friend's refrain of, "Pray continue". In the end I remained silent, and Mycroft went on.

"Early this evening I received a telegram from President Crump. I will read it to you. 'GREAT OPPORTUNITY FOR OUR TWO GREAT NATIONS. COME TO WASHINGTON TO SEAL THE DEAL.'"

"And you have no more information than that?"

"I do not but it is hard not to read this telegram in a positive light," said Mycroft holding up in his hand the piece of paper on which the telegram was written in what looked like a quite unwonted act of celebration. "This could mean that unlike other nations, we are tariff-free in our time. I want you, Dr Watson, to come to Washington to describe this diplomatic triumph in your own inimitable style."

"But this is an economic matter, and economics is not a subject in which I am in any way a specialist," said I cautiously.

"That is precisely why I have called upon you," replied Mycroft. "This country is tired of experts. If you laid all the economic experts in the world end to end, they still would not reach a conclusion. I need at my right hand someone who is not encumbered by their theories and prejudices so that he can proclaim the wonder of what has been negotiated in a way that the man on the street can understand. And," he added, "there is a train to Southampton in an hour and a liner sails from there at midnight. We will be across the Atlantic in five days."

There was something about the relentlessness and mastery that came from Mycroft's light grey eyes that made it impossible to resist any injunction from him and I went to pack my bag.

Throughout our journey the light of triumph never left his countenance.

"I am driven," he said at one point as he gazed out across the endless greyish expanse of ocean, "by something you wrote in *The Hound of the Baskervilles*."

I had passed to Mycroft the draft of this for his approval in 1889 although it had yet to appear in print. Nothing from it occurred to me that was relevant to what we were now engaged in, and I commented as much.

For answer Mycroft fished into a pocket and read out loud, " 'You may be cajoled into imagining that your own special trade or your own industry will be encouraged by a protective tariff, but it stands to reason that such legislation must in the long run keep away wealth from the country, diminish the value of our imports, and lower the general conditions of life in this island.'"

"But it was not I who said that," I objected. "And when your brother said it, he was reading out a leading article from *The Times* as part of our investigation into the Hound."

"Nevertheless, the sentiment is most admirable," replied Mycroft serenely.

Sooner than one might imagine, we had landed at New York and soon after that we were on a train to Washington. Throughout the journey Mycroft sat in almost complete silence, his eyes three quarters closed. I learned nothing of his contemplations which he interrupted only to take regular pinches of snuff.

Our liner had carried American newspapers which ranged from one to two weeks old, and I had spent my time reading up about American events of the time running up to our departure. On the train I now updated myself on the most recent events. The torrent of announcements from the new President on social matters, migrants, relations with other countries, and customs duties meant that the newspapers had plenty to write about.

I attempted to engage Mycroft in discussions on American politics but when I did so he confined himself to opening his eyes fully for an instant, and saying, "Mr Crump is doing what he said he would do before the Presidential election which he won with a comfortable majority. He therefore has a mandate from the American people for what he does for all that it is causing consternation among those who disagree with him."

He would then resume his previous serene expression.

It was striking how volatile the stock market had become. As one presidential announcement followed another, huge rises and falls in share prices had ensued. These were equal in magnitude to the objections raised by Crump's opponents to the policy announcements he was making. It seems harmless to confess now that my own share speculation had been driven by the opportunities I saw that this created.

We had no program for when we arrived in Washington. Indeed, for the first time in our acquaintance, Mycroft looked slightly sheepish when I asked him about it. In the end he admitted he had no agreed date for an appointment with the President. "We will have to wait until the President sends for us," he said. "I have no idea when that will be."

As we waited, I had time to open an account with a local stockbroker – the benefits of modern telegraphy meant that finding a stockbroker in Washington to trade on the Wall Street Stock Exchange in New York and on markets elsewhere was simplicity itself. The continued big rises and falls in stocks and shares made the possible profits to be made irresistible although

I knew that being short when an investment rose in price or long when it fell could have disastrous personal consequences.

When I signed up for my account, I saw that I was not the only person who realised the opportunity offered by the recent swings in the stock markets and I had to stand in a queue of people many of whom I would not expect to see at a stockbrokers in London – young, old, rich, poor, pale, swarthy. I noticed that even the distaff side was represented. They all gave reasons for their trade as they placed their trades, – "Tariffs on French wine will make US wine shares rise," "Dropping of tariffs on Russian furs mean American retailers become more profitable," were some of the opinions I heard, and they were backed by large sums of money.

After four days of waiting, the invitation to the White House finally came, and soon Mycroft and I stood before the President and his welcoming party.

While I had seen pictures of the new President before, they had all been in black and white. I noted now that he looked as though he had spent much time exposed to the sun. On one side of him stood his statuesque high-cheeked wife and on the other his bearded Vice-President, Mr Rance, with his slight wife who was I understood partly of native American descent although such descent is often erroneously referred to as Red Indian.

I think that Mycroft – like his brother, never fully at ease with social niceties – was quite relieved when the exchange of greetings between us was perfunctory. When we got down to business I was surprised when the women stayed in the room, but

Mycroft seemed to see no reason to object. As it was, it was the President who did most of the talking.

"So, Mr Holmes," began the President, "we see a great opportunity for our countries. Just as I have with so many other countries who have come here to seek a trade deal with me. But not all of them have listened to me."

"I am most pleased to hear it," said Mycroft cautiously.

"We would like to offer you in Britain free trade with nothing bothersome like customs tariffs levied. We would of course expect you to offer the same terms to us."

"In principle, Mr President, that is what we too are looking for. We would point out that in contrast to what is the case with many other countries, we buy more from you than you buy from us and a treaty of free trade will in all likelihood mean that that imbalance will grow…"

"And the price for us offering you free trade into our market – the biggest and greatest in the world – is," the President made a pause for emphasis, "Canada."

"I fear that I fail to understand you, Mr President," replied Mycroft, looking less than sure of himself, again a first in our acquaintanceship.

"Canada is a huge part of your Empire," continued the President, "and it is underdeveloped and unproductive. And that's just its people. It does nothing with its land which is mainly virgin forest or with what lies in the ground which is unexploited mineral deposits."

"Canada is still a young nation. All that will come when the time is ripe."

"The meek may inherit the earth, Mr Holmes, but not its drilling rights."

I do not think that Mycroft knew how to deal with this comment and there was a long silence before Vice-President Rance butted in.

"It would make much more sense if Canada became the latest and much-cherished state of the United States. In return for that we would let Great Britain have that tariff free trade we have talked about. And for Britain that trade would be with a larger country than what is at present one country and a British dominion. It would now be one country stretching all the way from Mexico to the Arctic and from the Atlantic to the Pacific," he said.

"It would be a win for us both," confirmed the President.

I watched Mycroft Holmes closely to see how he reacted and was reassured to see that he responded without blinking.

"The British Empire has always been governed by consent. We cannot simply hand over one of our peoples to you to secure a trade deal."

"Come, Mr Holmes. Every whore has a price."

I noted the President glance momentarily at his wife as he said this, and I stole a glance at Mycroft to see how he reacted to this unorthodox but pithy expression. Both Mycroft and Mrs

Crump seemed to my eyes to twitch uneasily at the President's provocative formulation.

"We would cut the Canadians' taxes and set them free to do our bidding."

"And what trading terms can you offer if there are difficulties for us in delivering up one of our dominions to you?" asked Mycroft still sounding uncharacteristically unsure of himself.

"If you don't agree with what I am proposing, we will hike your tariffs. Say 50% on everything we import from you. Would be great to see some foreigners paying our costs for a change rather than them living off us. We would call it 'Liberation Day'. And if you raise your tariffs on us, we will double our tariffs on you. How does that sound?"

"I fear I cannot agree to anything like that. If you wish, I can relay your offer to London and see what the response is."

"Before you arrived here, Mr Holmes, I had already arranged for your carriage at the back entrance of White House to be at the ready to take you back to your hotel for the eventuality that you do not agree with what I had to say. How about you go back there now? We might see you again when London tells you what you can agree with us," came the immediate reply.

Thus it was that in a much shorter time than I had anticipated that we climbed back into our carriage.

As we moved off, Mycroft looked utterly disconsolate, and, quite uncharacteristically, started talking our loud although I am not sure that he was addressing me. "What the President is looking for is quite impossible. What am I to say to the Prime Minister?" I was not sure if I was expected to respond to this and, when I noted that our carriage was passing my new stockbroker, I asked if I might descend. Mycroft remained silent. Whatever he meant by this silence, I took it as consent and got down. The carriage rolled on.

Difficulties in obtaining a free trade deal would push British stocks down, I reasoned, drawing on the inside knowledge I had gained from our meeting with the United States President. Indeed, for any exporter, the tariffs the President was proposing if Britain did not cede Canada to him would mean either that a higher price would have to be charged for the goods to the final user which would make them uncompetitive, or the exporter would have to absorb the costs in his chain of value and so become less profitable. And, I thought with a thrill in my heart, I was the only person who knew about it! There was as yet no way it could have got into the press. And being in Washington, with the wonders of modern communication, made no difference to my ability to trade on a distant stock exchange.

Accordingly, I decided to take out a future contract to sell shares in British Chemicals which I knew to be a major exporter of complex chemical preparations such as Epsom Salts, oven blacking, and brimstone to the United States. The contract was to sell at the current price in two weeks' time by which time the news of Mycroft's encounter with Mr Crump would have got out. I envisaged that the price drop by then would mean that selling at the current price but buying at the future price would yield me a handsome profit.

The stockbroker's office was again crowded when I went inside, and I stood in a long queue.

"You again," exclaimed the clerk in his booth to a tall dark man buying American gilts three places ahead of me in the line.

"With this President in charge, we will borrow more so bond prices will rise. I am buying them for a quick resale," I heard.

"I want to sell my stock in American Shipbuilders while they are at an all-time high. I think the President will cancel his tariffs on German ship builders and so ships will become cheaper," I heard a man with a broad southern accent say next. "It only stands to reason. I want to get out while the stock is at its high."

The slim youth in an ulster front of me shorted a company called American Lumber. "Trees are going become as cheap as chips when we take over Canada from Britain so the share price of American Lumber will fall," I heard. "The company's a dead man walking when new sources of supply become available. I'll sell them now and buy them cheap when it comes to the time for me to settle."

When it came to my turn, the clerk gave me a world-weary look. "Since we got the new President in, it has been one thing after another. First the French came, and French stocks dived. Then the same thing happened with the Germans. And now it's the turn of the British. It is all I can do to keep up with the volume of trades."

I would have liked to discuss matters further, but a queue was already forming behind me, so I felt unable to engage him in conversation. I placed my trade and returned to the hotel.

When I got there it was to my surprise that I found a note from Mycroft asking me to join him for dinner. When I got to the dining room it was to find that he had substituted his normal intake of snuff for the stubby, black-papered cigarettes he had smoked the first time I had met him in the matter I have described as *The Greek Interpreter*.

"What can I say to the Prime Minister?" he asked me, a rare note of plaintiveness in his voice. "He will do what I say – they all do – but the idea of surrendering our dominion over Canada is untenable. And what else will the United States President ask for if we cede Canada to him?"

I still felt on the crest of the wave after my share trade which I was sure would be a winner and replied, perhaps a little light-heartedly, "At least the volatility provides plenty of opportunity for the speculator."

Mycroft asked me to explain my remarks and I did so.

"And you have used your inside information here in Washington, doctor?" he asked.

"There is no such thing as insider information," I breezed. "Everyone is speculating as if shares were going out of fashion."

I recounted to Mycroft the full details of my trip to the stockbrokers and, rather to my surprise, he became more and more engaged as I went through my account of events. Indeed, so taken was he by it, that he asked me to repeat it adding any further detail I could recall. Once I had concluded, he relapsed once more into silence and smoked one cigarette after another but now with much more of his normal self-assurance.

Eventually he said, "Well, I suppose my brother failed to solve the Irene Adler case so why should I expect someone of even more limited ability than he to see through something similar? That case was about blackmail and so is this matter. Let us see what tomorrow brings."

The next morning the newspapers were full of accounts of Mycroft's meeting with the American President. Analysis was mixed with some papers regarding the treatment Mycroft got as revenge for the British torching of Washington in 1814 and others warning of the risks of antagonising one friendly nation after another. It was also mentioned that the next caller to the White House would be the Mexican leader who was to see the President that very morning.

I was surprised to be joined at breakfast by Mycroft who again puffed away at his little black cigarettes as he perused the newspapers.

To my even greater surprise he suddenly said, sounding much like his brother, "Be you ready at noon, good Doctor. We have an important matter to address at your stockbrokers."

The stockbrokers was only a short walk from the hotel but Mycroft, never a man to walk anywhere if he could help it, insisted on using a carriage to get there and I noted that he engaged the driver for the whole day.

He sat in his seat watching as a regular stream of would-be traders entered the broker's office. Suddenly I noted the young man in the ulster, who had the previous day shorted American Lumber, approach. I was about to say something when I realised that Mycroft was already descending to the street with a speed that was quite remarkable for one with so bulky a figure. I followed him as we stood behind the young man in the queue.

I heard him say, "I'd like to buy shares in the American Spice Manufacturers. Tariffs on Mexican spices will make American Spice more profitable."

As he turned to leave, Mycroft accosted him.

"Mrs Crump, all is known. Let us talk outside where our carriage awaits."

If I had any doubts about Mycroft's identification of the "young man" as Mrs Crump, the reaction to these words dispelled those doubts utterly. She staggered out onto the street and made no protest when Mycroft opened the door and helped her into our carriage where she sat opposite us.

"Like Irene Adler," said she, sounding breathless, "I am used to going out in men's clothing as I find it gives me more freedom to be anonymous."

"And I was expecting you to come here which is more than can be said for my brother when Miss Adler accosted him on the street and he failed to see through her disguise. I thus had an easy job of identification. I heard that there was a wild speculation on a fall in the share price of American Lumber before your husband's desire to take over Canada became public knowledge. If America takes over Canada, the supply of lumber to the American market will increase and prices will fall. When Dr Watson here told me that the trade had been placed by a slim young man in an ulster, the precise description he had given of the adventuress Irene Adler when she had disguised herself as a man in *A Scandal in Bohemia*, I knew that the would-be share speculator could only be you as only you knew of the President's plans. Why are you so in need of money?"

Mrs Crump took a deep breath, and it was quite a minute before she spoke.

"My husband is being blackmailed," she said at last. "His earnings as President are nothing like enough to cover what the blackmailer is asking."

"But your husband was a highly successful businessman before he became President."

"He had a lot of assets but no cash and that was disclosed in his tax returns. His companies are all illiquid."

"But tax returns are not public documents."

"No, but an agent of the Tsar of Russia somehow got hold of them. It was the fact that his businesses were out of cash that made my husband vulnerable to blackmail by the Russian leader."

The haughty eyes we had seen before suddenly looked needy and refused to return our gaze.

"But your husband has faced down scandal after scandal before."

She shrugged.

"That he may have had unwise associations was always impossible for the other party to prove beyond all doubt. When he was arraigned on criminal charges, they could be dismissed as being politically motivated. But official documents showing his true financial position were always going to be impossible to deny. The Russian leader knew that. He squeezed and squeezed demanding changes in policy and money. That was why my husband always said that the countries that the Tsar invaded got what they deserved."

"I can understand the announcements on political policy but what did the Russian leader want money for?"

"His predecessors have generally ended up being murdered. The idea was to build up a fund of money in the United States so that he could seek refuge here if matters took a difficult turn in Russia."

She went on.

"As my husband had nothing like the money to meet the demands, it was my idea that the President make outlandish pronouncements of policy which he then reversed. It maximised the possibilities for profitable speculation…"

"..Hardly speculation for you, dear lady, as you had prior knowledge of market sensitive data."

"Have you ever had to deal with a blackmailer?" Mrs Crump's eyes flashed angrily as she spoke. "He is sucking the life blood from us and every time we push a few million dollars in his direction, he asks for more."

By now our carriage had rattled into the precincts of the White House.

"I had better take you to see my husband."

It was just the four of us in the Oval Office and the President was shorn of the braggadocio he had exuded on our first visit to the White House as his wife explained what had happened.

"Well," he said to Mycroft, "you're supposed to be smarter than your brother and, to be fair, you seem to have proved it. How do we get out of this one?"

"I fear, Mr President, my responsibilities are confined to the interests of the British people and the British Empire."

"But that's huge. The sun never sets on it. What about me?"

"But it is British interests that I defend. And I can see no way of stopping the Tsar blackmailing you if what your tax documents say is true and he has them. But I will not publicise your share speculations as they are within the laws of the United States. And I see no evidence that your policy of making announcements and then rescinding them is making you unpopular."

Mr Crump seemed to have nothing to say to this and Mycroft continued.

"For my own country I would ask that you set tariffs at half the level of any other country and our tariffs will reflect yours. That will mean that some manufacturing comes here and that we shall gain some manufacturing that our rivals will put into British factories to benefit from the lower level of tariffs that we enjoy. And there can be no question of us ceding land to you in order to achieve such a deal."

"So you too are blackmailing me."

"I am defending the interests of my country and its Empire. And I rather share the Tsar's views about the likely outcome of his reign. I think a violent revolution will come at some point which will sweep him or one of his successors from power. For my part I have no power over him to stop him blackmailing you. The only option is for you to reveal your lack of commercial success…"

A look of defiance from the President revealed this was not acceptable to him..

"..and for now, as you say, it is not only the Tsar who knows about it. Apart from the people in this room."

The President started at this formulation and Mycroft went on.

"The only price I would seek for my silence would be for British interests to be taken into account in any future political announcements you make."

I have written up these notes on the ship on the way back from the United States. I have some clear ideas on future share speculations I might make.

At dinner on our last night at sea, Mycroft gave me an account of his *modus operandi*.

"I confess, good doctor, that I had always wandered about the President's habit of making dramatic policy announcements and then resiling from them. The President's way of working seemed to be of no real value to anyone, and the only beneficiaries were speculators such as yourself. You mentioned that you had seen someone shorting American Lumber before news of our first meeting with the president had been made public. That could only be being done by someone with inside knowledge of the President's plan to take over Canada. I realised what was happening as the description you gave fitted only Mrs Trump. I challenged her at your stockbrokers with the result that you saw. I must see what more I can do to exploit this opportunity for our country."

My readers will not have failed to notice that the person who gained the most from the denouement outlined above was the Russian leader who remains free to menace his country's neighbours and to benefit from the hold he has over the American President in any other way he chooses. I put this to Mycroft who shrugged.

"One can only make the best of the opportunities one has. I had an opportunity with the President and obtained what I think is the best available result for our country. If an opportunity arose with the Tsar, I would seek the same outcome."

I have read in the newspaper this morning that the President has been invited for a state visit to Britain.

While he is here, I have no doubt that Mycroft will take the opportunity to remind him of the need to make sure that British interests are taken into account on any political course he chooses to plot, and I can only see this country and its Empire benefitting.

Historical Note by Henry Durham, historical advisor to
***The Redacted Sherlock Holmes* series**

So outré are the events described that this episode of Mycroft's memoirs has been left as the last one in this volume even though the events described are dated to 1893 and so it would normally come between the account of the Ripper and the Dreyfus affairs.

That the American President of the 1890s should have been blackmailed by the leader of Russia – and, it is only fair to add, by Mycroft Holmes – is shocking and preposterous.

According to this account of events this blackmail seems to have driven American foreign policy as well as leading the American President's wife to speculate on shares with insider information in a way that would be completely illegal today.

We are fortunate that we live in better ordered times and that such a combination of events is now completely inconceivable.